Sara's journey

I was honored to read Patti's book *Sara's Journey*. I found the content captivating, the characters are so realistic and she stayed true to her religion. May we all find our way back.

—Bo Chiappa

My friendship with Patti goes back many years. In all the time I have known her, she has been a sweet and caring person. *Sara's Journey* takes place in Summerville, Georgia in the 1880's. The townspeople are all friends that go to the same church. They help each other out through the good times and bad with the power of God. As I was reading the manuscript, I noticed Patti put a little of herself in these characters. This is one recommended book not to be missed.

—Jessica Kain

Sara's Journey was a very touching book. It made me think of our dad. He was a great storyteller and loved good books and great stories. When Patricia and I were kids Dad used to tell us the best stories. Sometimes they were scary and sometimes funny I think that's why my sister is such a good writer and storyteller. She learned from the best—our Dad. If you read this book you won't be disappointed. I love you, Patricia, and Dad would be so proud of you...just as we all are. Love, your brother and number one fan...and I can't wait for your next book.

—Brian Leudeman.

I have known Patricia Ann Chiappa for practically my whole life. She is a wonderful person, a great writer, a good friend and my sister in law. She has a beautiful soul. My heart has been forever touched by reading *Sara's Journey*.

—Holly Lund

Very touching and heartfelt story; filled with faith.

—Glam Tam

Sara's journey

a novel

Patti Leudeman Chiappa

Sara's journey

a novel

Tate Publishing *& Enterprises*

The opinions expressed by the author are not necessarily those of Tate Publishing, LLC.

Published by Tate Publishing & Enterprises, LLC
127 E. Trade Center Terrace | Mustang, Oklahoma 73064 USA
1.888.361.9473 | www.tatepublishing.com

Tate Publishing is committed to excellence in the publishing industry. The company reflects the philosophy established by the founders, based on Psalm 68:11,
"The Lord gave the word and great was the company of those who published it."

Published in the United States of America

ISBN: 978-1-61663-299-1
1. Fiction / Christian / General   2. Fiction / General
10.04.21

Dedication

This book is dedicated to my hero and the best storyteller of them all: my dad. He was a man of courage, strength and kindness. I miss you dad. I also want to give special thanks to my mother, Audrey, and husband Anthony, because without their encouragement this book would never have been written. To the co-author of my book, Jesus Christ, I give all the praise and glory. I am only the messenger of your words. I dedicate this book to all the dreamers of the world—with Christ all things is possible. To Robert and Star Sweet, my friends who taught me how to let the light of Christ shine through me: I love you both. To Donna May, having you as my best friend and sister means having joy, laughter, love, faith, and understanding in my life. Thanks for always believing in me and supporting my dreams.

Foreword

BY AUDREY LEUDEMAN
& ANTHONY CHIAPPA

My three year old daughter, Patricia Chiappa, with her blonde curls and bright blue eyes, sat on my lap one lazy Sunday afternoon in her grandma Helen's back yard. She had just collected apples, in her radio flyer wagon, that had fallen from her grandmother's apple tree. "Wow, that's a lot of apples for you to eat alone," I said. Patricia smiled and replied, "I'm not gonna eat all the apples, Mommy. I'm gonna share them with God's children who dont have food to eat." From that moment on I knew my daughter would put the needs of others before herself. At a young age Patricia knew that man couldn't live by bread alone. My daughter, Patricia, her whole life has put the needs of others first, whether it be on her first day of kindergarten, when she befriended a boy who was being picked on by bullies, or donating her time by reading to the eldery at nursing homes, to putting on a fundraiser at her high school for her friend who had MS. Isn't that what God calls us all to do? Aren't we supposed to take care of each other? From an early age Patricia loved to write poems, songs, and stories. This has been her ministry for as long as I can remember. Patricia wants to write stories that empower the human spirit to encourage and to share God's love.

My love, Patricia, and I met while we were working together on a job site. For me it was love at first sight. I knew I would marry Patricia then and there. Our first date Patricia shared her faith with me. In her I saw an excitement, a spark, a fire and passion as she spoke of her love for the Lord. Patti prayed with me that night and I gave my life to the Lord. Patti, my love, has a very humble spirit. She is shy and she gives all the glory to God. Her favorite quote is, "Let the light of Christ shine in you, because somebody may be living in darkness and need your light to find their way home."

Chapter 1

Pastor Peter stood at the pulpit of his church on a beautiful fall day. The air inside the church was crisp and clean. If you looked outside the stained glass windows of the little white church, you could see all the leaves were painted with autumn's blush.

Pastor Peter looked around proudly at his faithful congregation. In the first pew sat the Miller family, the richest family in town. There was Kim Miller, a beautiful, classy woman in her thirties. She was a lean, tall woman with blond hair and blue eyes. There was her son, Little Ronnie, who was not so little. He was a young man with the strength of an ox. He had his father's good looks and his mother's gentle smile. Grandpa Miller sat beside his grandson Ronnie. Grandpa Miller was a good-looking older gentleman. He was tall and had brown hair and dark, mysterious eyes. They held much wisdom. Alongside of Grandpa sat Ronnie Miller, husband of Kim. He was a kind gentleman who never bragged about coming from a family of wealth. On the other end of the pew sat Mr. Fredrick, the farmhand of the Millers. Mr. Fredrick was a man of very little words. He was in his forties. No one knew his exact age. He was an immigrant from Poland. He worked for the Millers on their farm in exchange for free room and board. Mr. Fredrick lost his entire family in a horrible fire. He came to this small farming town, called Summerville Heights, to get a fresh start in life. Directly behind Mr. Fredrick in the second pew sat Anthony Joseph Grant. He was the fellow that ran the general store in town. He was a stocky man in his fifties. He was going bald. He wore thick heavy glasses. Next to him sat Sister Victoria. She was the oldest resident here, a beautiful older woman with a heart of gold. She would help anyone in need. The poor thing herself walked with a cane. She had a bad hip. Next to Sister Victoria sat Amy Carrie English. She was the wife of Pastor Peter. She was a stunning woman; she could have been a beauty queen. She had golden hair, blue eyes that were the color of the ocean, and legs that went on for miles and miles. On the other side of the church sat Old Doc Benson; he was the town's doctor. He was a man that was not only kind and gentle, but a man who, in spite of all his knowledge and wisdom, feared the Lord. He gave all his honor to God. Old Doc Benson was sixty years of age. He had pure-white hair and a beard to match. When Little Ronnie was a baby, he thought he was St. Nick. Next to him sat Helena Viola Smith. Helena was a plain but pretty lady in her late forties. She had a gift for cooking and making everyone around her feel comfortable. Everyone in town knew she was sweet on Mr. Fredrick.

Pastor Peter said, "Please, everyone, turn your hymn booklets to page sixty-eight as we honor our God and sing 'Amazing Grace.'"

Just as they started to sing, the door to the church opened with a squeak. Pastor Peter looked up with surprise. The rest of the congregation paid it no mind.

In walked a tall man with dark brown eyes and brown hair. He slipped into the back pew of the church.

Although Pastor Peter was annoyed at the man for coming to the service late, he stayed cool, calm, and collected.

After they finished singing "Amazing Grace," Pastor Peter asked them to take out their Bibles.

Although the pastor knew everyone in town, he did not know the mysterious stranger who had interrupted the service. As everyone reached for his or her Bibles, Pastor Peter couldn't help but gaze at the stranger. He noticed the stranger held in his hands a dirty, ripped, faded, old Bible.

Pastor Peter was very anxious to get to know who this stranger was. He had to focus all his thoughts on God. He asked the small but faithful congregation to turn to Corinthians 1:4. Then he read these words aloud: "I always thank God for you because of his grace given you by Christ Jesus for in him you have been enriched in every way, in all of your speaking and in your knowledge because our testimony about Christ was confirmed in you." Then Pastor Peter said a silent prayer to the heavens. As he was praying, he thought about his wonderful friends, how they all stuck together through good and bad times and how they enriched each other's lives. After his silent prayer, he did his sermon. After that, he blessed his congregation. He then invited them to share fellowship over a feast lovingly prepared by Helena. He was also very excited to talk to the stranger.

As they filed out of the church, the pastor stood by the door greeting each one of his friends with a handshake, smile, or warm embrace.

Suddenly he was standing face-to-face with the

stranger. The stranger extended his hand to Pastor Peter. Pastor Peter clasped his hand in the man's.

The stranger said, "Peace be with you, Pastor. I'm Turner Thomas."

Pastor Peter smiled at him and said, "I'm Pastor Peter. God's love be in your heart and welcome to our town." Pastor Peter then extended a personal invitation to share fellowship with them.

Turner replied, "Don't mind if I do. I have had a long journey. I am mighty hungry and tired."

Pastor Peter responded, "Come then; we will break bread together." Even though he had only known Turner for a few short minutes, he felt a warmth around him. Turner had rugged looks, but when he spoke, he spoke softly. The Pastor thought to himself his voice sounded like angel whispers.

They walked along the narrow path covered by fallen leaves of red, brown, and gold. Pastor Peter had so many questions he wanted to ask. Why was Tuner here? Where did he come from? Did he have family here? He did not want to overwhelm the newest member of Precious Blood United Methodist church.

The two men walked side by side in silence. It was just a few moments till they reached the run-down old building that they used to hold fellowship. Before they opened the doors to the building, they could smell the aroma of homemade banana bread, cranberry muffins, hazelnut coffee, and eggs.

Turner turned to the pastor. "That sure smells good."

Pastor said, "Wait till you taste it; it is a little taste of heaven on earth."

When the pastor opened the doors, he could see everyone sitting in their usual spots. The Millers, Mr. Fredrick, Old Doc Benson, and Helena at one table, and Sister Victoria, Anthony Joseph, and Amy at another.

Amy got up from her table. She walked over to greet her husband and the stranger. She turned to Turner and said, "I'm Amy, the pastor's wife. Please make yourself at home."

Turner said in reply, "I'm Turner Thomas. Pleased to meet you, miss."

Then she said, "Come sit down. May I get you something to eat?"

Just then Helena walked over with two plates. On the plates there were sweet-smelling slices of banana bread, fried eggs, fresh fruit, and homemade cranberry muffins. She handed one plate to the pastor and one plate to the man whose name she did not know yet.

"Please excuse me, miss, for not introducing myself. My name is Turner Thomas." She gave him a half-cocked smile and said, "Pleased to make your acquaintance. I'm Helena."

She heard the words coming from her mouth, but she couldn't believe she said them. What made Helena feel so at ease with the man she just met? She turned away from him with embarrassment in her eyes. "Excuse me," she said in a low voice. "I must attend to the others."

Pastor Peter, Turner, and Amy sat down together. All eyes in the room turned to the pastor as he said grace. As they lifted their heads after saying grace, they began to eat.

"Mmm, this is sure good. This is the best meal I've had in days," Turner said. "Thank you, Helena."

Helena, who was an earshot away, said, "You are welcome."

One by one, they came over to the stranger and introduced themselves to him. Turner felt comfortable with all of them. He also put them at ease.

After he finished his meal, he answered the questions on everyone's minds. Why was he here? Who was he? There was a hush among them as he began to tell his story.

"I am a missionary. I gave my life to Christ after my poor mother and father passed away of scarlet fever. I have walked for days to come to your town because God put a calling in my heart to come here."

They were all amazed and touched by his story and journey.

He continued to tell his life's story. "The last place I was in was a small town in the Appalachian Mountains. I have walked from there to here. On my way here, I met a kind family who gave me food and clothing for my journey.

Little Ronnie had tears in his eyes because this man Turner was the type of man he always admired. Little Ronnie admired turner for his quiet strength, his commitment to god, and the warmth that radiated off of turner. Ronnie wanted his life to reflect the goodness and love of god. He went on to say, "After my parents died, our little farmhouse was sold and I was sent to live with my aunt Millie for a while. When she died, I had no family left. My Aunt Millie gave me her old Bible on her deathbed. After her death, I began to read it and I found Christ. That's when I started my life as a missionary."

Old Doc was so touched by his story he had to look away so the others would not see the tears in his eyes.

Grandpa Miller then asked, "Where are you staying while you are here?"

Turner said, "Well I was hoping there was a boarding house nearby"

Ronnie then said, "Nope; the nearest one is in Gingerbread Landing, and that is nearly fifty miles away. We have a spare room. You are welcome to stay in it while you are here."

"Thank you for the hospitality. You all know how to make a weary traveler feel welcomed," Turner said.

Then Sister Victoria noticed it was getting dark. The fall wind was angry. Sister Victoria said, "All of us better be going if we want to make it home before dark." They all agreed.

As Pastor Peter opened the door, the howl of the wicked fall wind ripped through their skin like bullets. The woman huddled together to keep warm while the men went to get the horses.

Old Doc left right away on his horse, Healer. Anthony left next on his black horse, called Little Friend. Then Pastor Peter and Amy left on their horse Heaven's Light. Old Faithful gently took Sister Victoria home.

Suddenly the Millers stood alone with Turner. Little Ronnie pulled up in front of them with a beautiful carriage led by two beautiful stallions. One horse had a shiny black coat and a full mane. They called that horse Liberty. The other horse was an older stallion of brown color called Freedom.

Grandpa Miller helped Kim in the carriage first and then got in himself. Then Little Ronnie and Turner followed by Mr. Miller. Ronnie took the reins of the horses, and with one gentle slap on the backside of Liberty, he led the horses into a steady gallop toward home.

As they rode the twisted roads and lanes of the countryside, Turner took in the town's understated artistry. There was a small cottage hidden behind tall oak trees, a cozy little town square with a general store and Doc Benson's office. There was a little flowing stream that separated the main road in town from a path up the mountainside. As they drove, Grandpa Miller gave Turner a town history lesson. Turner then spotted an ice cream parlor and then said, "No one told me you had an ice cream parlor here!"

"Yes, Mrs. Ruth Brown runs it," Mr. Miller said. "You won't see her too much while you are here. She doesn't go to church or socialize. You only may see her if you stop there to get a cone.

Grandpa Miller added, joking, "She has delicious ice cream though; that's where I got all my extra padding from."

They all laughed. Suddenly their moods turned more somber and silent. Turner could only guess why. He did not question them about it; none of them gave an explanation. He did notice as they passed a burnt-out little cottage that their moods had changed. They all sat silently for the rest of the way home.

"Well, this is it," Mrs. Miller said. "This is where we call home, plain and simple," Grandpa Miller added.

Turner could not understand for the life of him why they called the home plain and simple. This house was more breathtaking than any house Turner had ever seen. It had a fishing pond, a wraparound porch, and a garden of red, green, yellow, pink, and purple roses. From the outside, not even stepping foot into it, he could see this was not an ordinary home.

When Mr. Miller turned the door handle to walk inside, they were met with the fragrance of sweet-smelling perfumed roses. On the table of fine craftsmanship sat a hand-painted vase. Inside the vase there were several different kinds of flowers. Next to the vase was a hand-painted teapot and cups. Turner noticed on the table there was a fine lace tablecloth that must have been passed down from one generation to the next. In the middle of the huge room was a stone fireplace. Turner stood in awe as he looked around the room. On the wall he saw a painting of a glorious woman.

"That's my late wife," Grandpa Miller said. "She died giving birth to Ronnie."

Turner said, "God gives us blessings and trials to make us stronger." He couldn't help notice the affection in Grandpa Miller's voice as he spoke of his late wife.

Then Mrs. Miller said to break the sadness in the room, "Let me show you the rest of the house and where you can wash up. I'll make you something to eat; then you can rest. You must be tired from the events of today." She asked her husband to give Turner the grand tour. It had three bedrooms and indoor plumbing, a luxury in those days.

Mrs. Miller was busy in the kitchen preparing chicken and greens. She set the table elegantly for their guest. The finest meal and china they could offer.

Grandpa Miller led them in prayer. After they ate, they retired for the evening to their feather beds. Turner stayed in the guest room. It was, of course, more than he had ever dreamed. It had a feather bed; on the bed were silk linens and a hand-sewn quilt. On the right side of the room, there was a fireplace. On the left side, there was a mahogany desk with a chair and a dresser. On top of the dresser, there were to candles lit. A lantern was hanging on the bedpost. There was a comb and brush, fine powders, and aftershave. *The Millers must only keep this room for special guests,* he thought. He opened his Bible and began to read. Then a thought came rushing through his mind. *Could the Millers know his secret?* Panic set in his heart, but God quickly rushed it away. He was tired. His body was achy. He blew out the candles and settled into the big, cozy bed. As soon as he hit the pillows, his mind and body drifted into a peaceful sleep.

The next morning the dawn's sunlight broke through the windows of the little happy home. Mr. Miller and Little Ronnie were already out working the farm. Grandpa Miller had taken Freedom and Liberty to the general store to get materials and sewing supplies for Kim. Christmas was coming, and Kim wanted to make a special gift.

Kim was busy making oatmeal and hotcakes for breakfast. As the dawn turned to full sunlight, Turner felt the warmth on his face and it awoke him. He threw his legs over the bed and onto the cold floor. He threw on his boots and a borrowed a tan pair of pants that was lent to him by the family he met coming here. He then put on a red flannel shirt. He took out of his bag containing his few belongings. He got washed and shaved. He then stepped out into the room where Kim had once again set a pretty table for their breakfast.

"Good morning. Did you sleep well?" Kim asked in a cheery voice.

"Quite well, thank you," he said in reply.

"The boys are just getting washed up. They will be joining us in a few moments. After we eat, the boys will give you a tour of our land and take you into town. I'm sure there are a few things that you will need while you are here."

"Yes." He could barely get out a thank you when the men came.

"Fit for a king," Ronnie said as he looked lovingly at his wife.

"Why, Mr. Ronnie Miller, you make me blush," she said in a happy, spirited voice.

"Maybe our guest would like to lead us in a prayer," Grandpa Miller suggested.

Tuner responded, "It would be my honor."

They closed their eyes and bowed their heads.

Turner quietly spoke. "Dear Father, thank you for my new friends, this delicious food, and once again, I humbly offer my heart to you."

As he was speaking, Little Ronnie opened his eyes. He looked at Turner. He almost saw a light around him. No, his mind was playing tricks on him. After the blessings, they had their fill of hot cakes, oatmeal, and mouth-watering biscuits.

After they ate, they cleared the dishes away and the men got the horses ready to take a drive to town.

When they entered the stable, Mr. Miller said, "Oh, I almost forgot. I promised you a tour of the farm."

"Yes, a tour. I would love to see it," Turner said.

"Well, this is the stable. You know Freedom and Liberty," he said.

"Yes, I met them yesterday," Turner said in a laughing manner.

"On the other side of this path is our chicken coop. We have ten chickens, four hens and a rooster. Down a ways on the dirt path you will come to the field where our cows graze. We have four of them we use for milk. Old Bess we get the best milk from. We have our pond; the water comes from the mountaintop that we showed you yesterday. We have lots of catfish in there. We will go fishing sometime."

Grandpa Miller also added, "In the back woods, you can find lots of bear and deer. We will take you hunting someday."

"I'm not much of a hunter, I'm afraid. My father tried to pass his skills on to me, but he passed away too early in life to finish teaching me," Turner said.

"Then I'll teach you," Little Ronnie said joyfully. Proudly, he added, "I shot the bear that we got the bear skin rug from. I surprised Mama with it on her last birthday."

"Quite an accomplishment," his father said proudly. Turner nodded in agreement.

"Well, I think we'd better head into town now," Ronnie said.

They walked back to the stable. Then Mr. Miller and Little Ronnie hooked Freedom and Liberty up to the wagon. They all climbed in and headed toward town.

"What was that?" Turner asked with confusion. He couldn't believe his eyes. "Was that a woman I saw in that burnt-out shell of a house?" he asked with heavy sadness.

No one looked at him. They looked away. Then with a broken voice, Grandpa said, "I'm afraid so."

Turner continued to question him about the woman. "How could a woman live in that condition? Who was she? Did she have family? Anyone who cared?"

Before anyone could answer his questions, he offered a prayer to God. The men told him the sad story of that woman's existence.

Grandpa said, "Her name is Sara Wilson. She's lived in that house all her life with her parents until her seventeen year. That's when she met a handsome young man named Larry Frank. He was very charming and charmed his way into her heart. Her parents thought there was something odd about him, so when he asked her father for his daughter's hand in marriage in her eighteenth year, he told him no. She loved him and wanted to be with him. They ran away to Tennessee to get married." Grandpa paused with a tear in his eye. He could no longer speak of the tragedy.

Little Ronnie, eager to share the history of the townspeople, told the rest of the story. "After they got married, her mom did not receive word from her. Her mom died of a broken heart. It was not until Sara received word that her dad became ill that she returned home. Her father and Sara reconciled. For the love of Sara, he accepted her love of Larry." He had to stop for a moment to swallow a big lump in his throat. Then Little Ronnie lowered his voice and said, "Daddy, can you tell the rest of the story?"

Ronnie looked at his son and said, "I think we have said too much already."

Turner looked at the three grown men and saw the sadness in their eyes. He did not force them to speak of Sara further. He tried to lighten the mood by talking about the items he needed at the store.

Chapter 2

They soon reached the town square where the general store was located. Ronnie got out first and tied the horses to a post. The other men followed.

When they walked into the general store, they saw Old Doc Benson there. He was there buying ginger treats. When he saw the men, he exchanged pleasantries with them. He said to them, "Please don't think I'm being rude, but I have a patient I have to go check on."

The other men gave him a look of understanding. They said goodbye to each other. Old Doc walked out of the store.

Turner looked around the small one-room store. Behind the counter on a stool sat Anthony Joseph. The two men waved to each other. At the far end of the store was a small shelf full of sewing supplies. Underneath that shelf were farming supplies, seeds, dirt, mulch, and fertilizer. Directly in front of the counter where Anthony sat were penny candies, cigarettes, and cigars. On the other end of the store, there were fruits and vegetables, mostly supplied by the Millers' farm. The small store also doubled as the post office. Anthony also ran it.

Turner wanted to repay the Millers for their hospitality. While at the store, he got the Millers some seeds for their garden. Meanwhile, Grandpa Miller and Little Ronnie were getting some seeds and fertilizer they needed for the farm. Ronnie was getting pennies for Kim because she had a sweet tooth.

Turner also got some shaving cream, a razor, and socks. Mr. Miller also surprised Turner by purchasing a new pair of boots for him. Turner said to Ronnie, "No I couldn't take that; you have done so much for me already."

Ronnie insisted on getting him the boots.

Turner was overwhelmed with his kind gesture that he could not find the words to say thank you.

Ronnie could read his heart and saw the emotion in his eyes. So the two men exchanged no words, but instead smiled at each other. Before they paid for their goods, Anthony said to Grandpa Miller, "The material and sewing supplies you ordered for Kim have just arrived."

Mr. Miller said, "What do we owe you for it?"

Anthony replied, "Just bring me some eggs and milk tomorrow, and we will call it even."

Ronnie shook Anthony's hand and said, "It's a deal."

The other men took the bags of the items and loaded it into the wagon.

Grandpa Miller said, "Before we head on home, I'd like to go check on Sister Victoria today."

Little Ronnie added, "Yes, I think her hip is troubling her again."

The men loaded into the wagon.

Ronnie turned to Turner and said, "Now you are going to see some really pretty sights because we are going halfway up the mountain."

Turner said, "I will enjoy the ride."

With a clap of his wrists on Liberty, the two horses began to pull the wagon.

Turner couldn't help but be thankful to God for his outstanding artwork. Everywhere he looked he could see God's handprint. On the way to Sister Victoria's house, the men made small talk. Turner sat half listening and half daydreaming. He was too interested in what he saw around him to concentrate on what the men were talking about. Turner saw a deer drinking from a babbling brook, beautiful apple orchards, a little boy playing with a black and white pup; fallen leaves painted the ground with brilliant bright colors, of red, gold, and earth tones.

"Turner, Turner," Ronnie said.

"Oh, I'm sorry. I've just been admiring God's handiwork," Turner said.

The men laughed. "Happens every time you are here you are in the presence of God," Grandpa said.

Ronnie said, "A man could disappear in God's magic here. I just wanted to tell you we have arrived at Sister Victoria's house."

The cottage was a happy looking one. Although it was small, Turner could feel all the warmth, joy, and love it held.

Outside of the cottage under a large oak tree, two women sat drinking sweet tea. One woman Turner knew as Sister Victoria; the other he did not know.

The men approached the women. "Why, good day, gentlemen," Sister Victoria said.

The young woman Turner didn't know sat silently.

"Good day to you ladies also," Ronnie said.

Sister Victoria offered each of the gentlemen a glass of

sweet tea. Then she introduced Turner to Ann Smith. She was the schoolmarm of Summerville Heights.

"Pleased to make your acquaintance," Turner said.

"How do you do?" she said in reply. They all sat for a while outside until it turned to cold.

Sister invited everyone inside. When they got inside, Grandpa Miller took the Liberty of building a fire. The cottage was very small. It was clean and pretty.

Ronnie then said to Sister Victoria, "We just came to check on you to see if you needed anything and offer you a ride to see Doc about that hip of yours."

Sister Victoria paused for a moment then said, "I do appreciate the kind offer, but Anna had just brought me sliced ham and apple cider. Earlier today her husband took me to see the Doc."

Ronnie was relieved. He then realized Sister must have been the patient Doc rushed off to see.

It got warm inside the small cottage by the fire Grandpa Miller had built. They sat around a small wooden table. They chatted for a bit. Ann then said, "Would anyone like a cup of tea?"

"Sounds good," Sister said. "I'll help you."

Over the fire she warmed up tea from that morning's breakfast. She also put a tin of butter cookies on the table.

As they talked, Ann remarked on how big Little Ronnie had gotten since she had begun teaching him ten years ago.

Sister then said, "Has anyone been over to leave food on Sara's doorstep?" Suddenly she realized that Turner was in the room, and she refrained from saying any more.

Grandpa Miller then said, "Sister, you do not need to

talk of Sara in whispers around Turner. We saw her peering through her window yesterday."

Turner saw the joy that danced in the room among these friends just a few moments ago disappear.

Ronnie then turned to Turner and looked him straight in the eye. He then said, "There is something you need to know."

"Hush now, you hear! Hush!" The normally soft-spoken woman had fury in her voice. Grandpa Miller gently touched her hand and said, "He needs to know."

"Well," she said, "if you want to tell him, I have to leave. I can't bear to listen to this. I've seen it is firsthand." The two women left the room where the men were sitting.

"Tell me? Tell me what?" Turner said with a nervous voice.

Grandpa Miller hung his head low. His eyes filled with dark shadows as he told the story of Sara. "She was so full of life, so enthusiastic; she wanted to be a dancer."

Turner could see the tears welling up in his eyes but tried to pretend he did not.

Grandpa went on. "After Sara returned home with her husband, everyone seemed so happy. Sara joined the church committee, held Bible study, and even became a midwife for Old Doc. She never gave up on her dancing either. She took care of her father. As her father became gravely ill, Larry became cruel and cold. Some of the town folk overheard him talking one day that he couldn't wait for him to die so he could have his wife all to himself. People began staying away from them. Shortly after Sara's father died, she changed. She stopped going to church, gave up dancing, and stopped growing her flowers. Some say it was because she was mourning her late father, but the town people soon learned the truth was far worse. Her husband began drinking and beating her. Sara always said she fell or tripped or something like that. At night, you could hear her blood-curdling screams. Everyone in town knew her husband was hitting her. But every time the law came to check on her she said he wasn't. One night the townspeople made a plan to get Sara to safety. They were going to scare her husband as a payback for what he did to her. The men got together, myself and Ronnie included. We all went to Sara's house. Ronnie and I were the first ones there."

Grandpa Miller could no longer hide his tears of pain. He broke down and sobbed like a newborn baby.

Turner, in a comforting move, put his hand on Grandpa's shoulder. Turner's touch was such a comfort to him. "Ronnie, tell him the rest," he said between sobs.

Ronnie said with a weak childlike voice, "When we got to the house, it was on fire."

Turner could hear the panic in his voice like he was reliving that painful memory.

"Dad and I rushed through the burning flames to only find Sara. Larry had slipped out under the cover of the night. I could taste Sara's burning flesh in my mouth as I carried her to the safety of her yard. When Doc arrived, he rushed Sara to Gingerbread Landing. There they have a special hospital where they treat burn victims. It was too late. Sara survived, but her face was disfigured forever. When Sara awoke, she couldn't remember anything about the fire. The law tried to find Larry but never did. Old Doc Benson has been the only person to see her face since she was released from the hospital. Doc Benson, being the kind man he is, took Sara in and treated her like a daughter, but Sara never recovered physically or mentally. She returned to her burnt home because she blamed herself for what happened." Ronnie almost collapsed on the floor after telling Sara's story.

From the other room, he heard the two women weeping. He could see that Little Ronnie was shaking. Turner tried to comfort all of them with prayer. He said this Scripture from Psalms: "The righteous cry and the Lord hears them, he delivers them from all their troubles, the Lord is close to the brokenhearted and saves those who are crushed in spirit."

Suddenly a wave of peace came over them all. Grandpa Miller then said, "You are a Godsend, Turner." The women who were kneeling in the doorway during the prayer rose to their feet. They dried their eyes. Turner looked at them compassionately.

Ann then said, "The women of the town take turns making food for Sara. She will not allow us to see her, so we leave it on her doorstep. Old Doc Benson comes weekly to check on her too. Kim is talented in sewing, so every Christmas she makes Sara a new dress."

It was now Turner that was filled with emotion. He needed to let his emotions out. He turned and cried.

Sister Victoria then said, "There is no need for us to live in the past. With God's help, we will all find a way to help Sara."

Ann said to Ronnie, "It is getting late. Won't Kim be worried about you?"

"Yes, I think we better get going," he said. The men thanked Sister Victoria and then left.

All the way home the men neither looked at each other nor talked. They were too wrapped up in their own thoughts to do either. As they passed Sara's house, Turner prayed deeply for her.

Kim had a look of worry on her face. She ran to her husband and kissed him.

"I was worried sick. When the lunch hour came and went, I sent Fredrick out looking for you." Before she could finish, Ronnie explained the events of their day. "Well, I'm just glad you are all home."

Mr. Fredrick agreed with her. They all sat down to eat. Mr. Fredrick said grace. Even in his broken English, they all understood his language of love.

They were enjoying the soup Kim had made. They were just finishing dinner when there was a knock on the door. It was Forest Smith.

Chapter 3

"Come in, come in," said Ronnie. As he stood by the open doorway, he could feel the night air brush his cheek.

Forest could hardly contain the joy and excitement on his face.

"What brings you by this late hour?" Ronnie said to him.

Kim then said, "Should I leave is this business among men or friends?"

"No, don't leave. This concerns all of you," he went on.

They all looked at him with puzzled faces. "My wife and I got word from Old Doc Benson today. We are expecting our first child," he said happily.

All at once they made a cheer that could have woken their relatives sleeping in eternal rest.

The Miller and Smith families had known each other for ages.

"Wait, wait, wait. There's more. You haven't heard the best part yet. Ronnie, because you are like a brother to me, the wife and I would like you and Kim to be godparents!"

Kim leaped off her seat and ran over and hugged him.

"Little Ronnie, we don't want to leave you out. Ann and I would like you to help pick out the baby's christening name."

Little Ronnie jumped so high he almost hit his head on the ceiling.

Mr. Fredrick said, "Let's pray." Everyone knew what he meant. They all joined hands together

Ronnie led them in prayer. From Psalms 115, he prayed, "The Lord remembers us and will bless us. He will bless who fear the Lord; may the Lord make you increase, you and your children. May you be blessed by the maker of heaven and earth."

After they prayed, Ronnie called for a celebration.

Forest said, "I'm sorry I can't stay. I have to get home to Anna."

Kim then said, "We understand, but you and Anna must come over on Thanksgiving evening to celebrate."

He said, "We will." They all hugged him. It turned into a bear hug. As he rode away on his horse, even under the night sky they could see the joy beaming from his eyes and Hope for the future extending from his smile.

The night was long. Everyone was too excited to sleep. They lay awake in their feather beds.

Little Ronnie found a sheet of paper in his desk. He started to write down baby names. Kim lay awake planning the celebration dinner. Grandpa laid awake drawing pictures in his mind on the newest member of Summerville Heights. Ronnie lay awake staring at the stars, thanking God for this miracle. Turner laid awake thinking about Sara. Yes, he was happy for his new friends, but he couldn't get Sara, the lost sheep, out of his mind. He prayed for Sara all night until Turner's eyes that were turned to heaven were too heavy to stay awake.

Night turned to day. Little Ronnie awoke at the break of dawn to help his dad as he always did on the farm. Mr.

Fredrick was already outside milking old Bessie. Kim was working in the kitchen.

Turner went outside. He took in a deep breath of the cold air. He saw birds gathering flying south for the winter. Squirrels were hiding their nuts.

"Hello, Ronnie" he said.

Ronnie turned around. His face was red from the fall air. "I'm glad you are up. Would you like to go hunting?"

Turner was not much for hunting. He did not want to insult his host." he said. "I can't promise you I'll kill anything."

Ronnie didn't question what he meant. "First, we will have breakfast. Little Ronnie and Grandpa ate already today. They went into town with Mr. Fredrick to get some oats and hay."

They enjoyed the breakfast Kim made. They enjoyed a breakfast of hot bread, strawberry jam, and grits. Ronnie said to Turner, "Before we go outside, I'll give you a warmer coat. It's going to get cold out there."

Turner said, "Thank you." He slipped the coat on that Ronnie gave to him.

Ronnie picked up two guns. "Here, you use this one. It is easier to aim."

Turner hated holding a gun in his hands but remained silent.

They walked deep into the woods. Right away Ronnie spotted a young fawn. "Tonight's dinner," he said to Turner. He aimed, but she got away.

Turner was secretly happy. They waited in the bush for what seemed like hours. There was not another deer in sight. Ronnie suddenly spotted a wild pig. He pulled back the trigger and aimed. Turner looked away. "I've got him!" Ronnie said proudly. He went to where the pig laid. He put it on his shoulders. He and Turner walked out of the woods.

"Honey, we are home. Mr. Fredrick and I got what we needed from the store," Grandpa Miller called to his daughter-in-law.

Just then, Turner and Ronnie returned with the fat, bloody pig around his neck.

"Good, you are all home just in time for lunch. Put that pig down and get washed up," Kim said.

"Yes, Mama," they all said in reply.

"What's on the menu for today?" Ronnie said to his wife in a happy mood.

"It's a surprise," she said.

"Whatever it is, it sure smells good." Little Ronnie's voice seemed to appear out of nowhere.

"What have we done to deserve a delicious meal like this?" Grandpa Miller asked.

On the beautifully set table there was a turkey with corn bread dressing, corn, peas, and an apple pie.

"This is mouth-watering," Turner added.

This time Kim herself said grace. "Dig in," she said. They sure did. Kim made a special meal in honor of their new friend Turner.

• • •

It was late afternoon when Turner told his friends he was going for a walk. He needed some time alone to pray, meditate, and think. In his heart, he knew the mission he was sent on would be difficult, but he would not fail. As he walked, he stopped dead in front of Sara's house. He could not see Sara, but he knew she was there. He could not turn away from the shell of the blackened house even though his heart broke when he thought of man's ugliness. He could see the tall grass that hid the front of the house. It was almost like the blades were hiding Sara's shame. The front windows had cloth over them, as well as the back ones, to hide Sara from the world. The roof had been burnt just a little, so that was one blessing Turner found in this tragedy. He thought to himself, *At least she is shielded from the elements.* He could see apple trees that were rotting away, limbs of mighty oaks and maples that had fallen from years of neglect. He could see two small head stones planted near a lilac bush. His curiosity got the best of him, so he went in for a closer look. One was bearing the name Mary Wilson; one was baring the name Vincent Wilson. "Undoubtedly Sara's parents," he said aloud.

Suddenly he heard a voice of a woman. "Get out of here! What do you want with me? Leave me alone!" The voice was filled with bitterness, anger, and sadness.

"Could it be? Could it be Sara?" He turned around with one swift motion. His eyes focused on the house. He could not see her but knew her voice.

"Well, answer me!" the voice shouted again.

Turner prayed a quick prayer to find the right words to break the fortress of her broken heart. "I'm Turner Thomas," he said.

"I don't care who you are. Just leave me be!" the voice sounded more fearful now.

"I'm not here to hurt you. I just got into town yesterday. I'm a missionary. If there is anything I can do to help you, let me know."

She spoke in a softer, calmer voice now. "Pastor gives me all the prayers I need. I get all my food and clothes I need from the town. I don't need any more help. Please leave and don't come back."

Turner had an idea. At the moment, he would have to leave, but he would be back. As he turned from the house, he could almost feel her eyes burn through him.

• • •

Inside the blackened house, Sara's own tears were burning her eyes and face. "Why, God, why did you do this to me? I was your faithful servant, and this is how you repay me by abandoning me in my greatest hour of need?" Her prayer was so pitiful and sad; she collapsed on the floor from crying so much. She used all her strength begging god for an answer!

• • •

Turner continued down the county road called Happiness Trail. He could not help but think how ironic it was that the main road in town was called Happiness Trail when so much pain, heartbreak, and sorrow happened here. As he traveled down the road, he heard birds singing. He thought to himself, *Is it God reminding me that he will give us beauty for our ashes?* He stopped for a while and sat on a large rock. He was a little tired, but he wanted to stop and talk to God. "God, please help me be the person Sara needs me to be so I may restore her faith in mankind and help her to see the beauty in herself." He got off the rock and kept walking.

He soon found himself in the middle of the town square. He wanted to go talk to Doc about Sara. He walked in the doors to Doc's office. Inside there were three chairs he used as a waiting room. Just behind that there was a door, leading to the exam room. On one of the chairs sat one of the ladies he met at church. It was Helena.

"I just can't get rid of this cold, so I've come to Doc's office for him to make a mustard rub for my chest and give me some castor oil. I Hope you're not sick from your journey," Helena said.

"No, Helena. I just came to see Doc," Turner said.

Helena said, "He should be out in a moment."

Soon the door to the exam room opened. From it came a woman he didn't know. Later he found out it was Ruth Brown.

"Next," the Doc called. Helena went in after saying goodbye to Turner.

Turner waited patiently until he was called back to the exam room. Doc shook his hand. "Well, hello. I'm surprised to see you Turner, are you sick?"

Turner said, "Well, no not exactly, but I am sick in my heart." Turner was wearing a distressed look on his face.

"This must be serious," Doc said.

Turner replied, "Yes, it is. It's about Lady Sara."

Old Doc's face turned gray. If his hair could have gotten any whiter, it would have at the mention of Sara's name. "Please, don't get involved. It will only cause you pain."

"She is a child of God, and I am a missionary. I am involved." Turner's voice was filled with righteous anger.

"Please don't misunderstand. I love Sara; that's why I don't want to see her get hurt. Let me explain. A few years back a new minister rode into town before Pastor Peter came here. He too wanted to help Sara. When she started trusting him, she found out he was no minister at all; he was a con artist, trying to take advantage of Sara. He thought she had a dowry." Doc's eyes lowered with grief.

"That's horrible," Turner said. "I would never hurt Sara like that."

"You know that and I know that, but Sara doesn't know that." Doc drove home that point with strength in his voice. "There is something else no one knows about Sara. I'm telling you because I trust you. At the time of the fire, Sara was with child."

Turner needed to know, so he asked, "Did the child survive?"

"No, she didn't," Doc answered.

Before Turner could speak or react to that answer, Doc said, "Come; there is something I want to show you."

Turner tried to hide his sadness as he followed Doc out of the back door of his office. Old Doc lead him to a stable that was between his office and the general store.

"Come, look here," Doc said.

Turner tried to hide his disappointment when all he saw was horses. He thought Old Doc would hold the key to winning Sara's trust.

"Here, come look!" Doc called out again. "This is my horse, Healer. This is Ruth Brown's horse, Candy Apple, and this, my friend, is Sara's horse, Morning Dew."

Sara had a horse? Turner thought to himself with surprise.

"Sara's father got her this horse on her twenty-first year birthday, after she came home. Sara loved this horse so much. After the fire, like all other things she loved, she gave him up, but she did make me promise to take care of Morning Dew. I have many patients, and sometimes I cannot always look after Morning Dew for her. Would you help me take care of the horse for her while you are here?"

"Yes, of course I will. It will be a great honor," Turner said.

Just then they saw Mr. Frederick riding up the road on Freedom. As he approached the two men, he had a panicked, urgent look on his face. "Doc! Come quick! Something is wrong with old Bess and all the other cows," he said breathlessly.

Dr. Benson threw the saddle on Healer, and Mr. Frederick told Turner to quickly get on Freedom, and the three men raced toward the Miller farm.

When they got to the farm, everyone was in a panic. Grandpa was out with old Bess. Little Ronnie and Ronnie were trying everything to make the cows feel better. Kim was in the house crying and pacing the floor just like a worried mommy.

Old Doc Benson examined old Bess first. He could hear through his stethoscope her breathing was shallow and her rapid heartbeat. When he examined the other cow, he heard the same thing. He whispered to Turner, "They probably won't make it through the night."

Grandpa, in all his years working on the farm, had never seen anything like this. If they lost the cows, they would lose a big chunk of their livelihood. The whole town would be without milk. The family watched helplessly as the cows got sicker and sicker. Old Doc couldn't do anything for them. He knew before dawn the cows would be dead.

"Wait, is there a vet over in Gingerbread Landing that might help us?" Kim said.

"Yes, but it will take two days before they can get

here, and I am afraid it will be too late," Ronnie said sadly. Through the night they kept watch over there sick and dying cows. Sadly, one by one, their heartbeats stopped. They cried.

Grandpa Miller said, "There is nothing more we can do tonight. God will somehow provide for us." They said a prayer for their loving cows.

Kim said to Doc, "It's too late for you to go home. You will stay here tonight." With achy bodies smelling of grass and cows, they tried to sleep.

The next morning things were very silent in the Miller home. Kim prepared breakfast with a heavy heart.

Mr. Frederick came into the house holding a piece of paper in his hands. He could not read or write, so he showed no emotion when he handed it to Ronnie. It was a note from Turner. He announced to everyone, "My dearest friends, I'm sorry I seem so cold, but I must leave you for a while. I am sorry I couldn't say goodbye in person. Love Turner."

Turner was gone. How could this man they grew to love so much leave them in their hour of need? After all they did for him, to leave without an explanation? No tears, no goodbyes.

Ronnie threw the letter down and stormed out the door. Kim stood in shock; she was unaware that breakfast was burning on the stove. Little Ronnie ran to take breakfast off the stove. Mr. Frederick and Doc were completely dumbfounded. Old Doc couldn't believe after the bond they formed and Sara's secret he shared that Turner could leave and not look back. He wouldn't even get to spend Thanksgiving with them if he was not back soon.

After a few moments alone, Ronnie got his wits about

him. He said to his family, "We should pray that no matter where Turner is going, he has a safe journey. Dear Lord, please protect Turner. Let him know our love goes with him, and if he does not return, please let him know we are grateful for the time we had with him."

They ate breakfast in silence that morning for the first time since Grandma had passed away.

In town, news was traveling fast that just as the mysterious stranger appeared he left. Everyone was devastated. When they heard the news of the cows' deaths, they were also worried where they would get their milk. Anna was especially worried now that she was pregnant.

Ruth had a small goat that was very old and did not produce much milk. When she heard the cows died, she showed compassion to her neighbors and shared her goat's milk. All the neighbors tried to save their milk to give to Anna.

• • •

Weeks passed with no word from Turner. People wondered if he was really a friend at all.

It was Sunday, November 22, the Sunday before Thanksgiving. Pastor Peter was working on his sermon. All the townspeople were dressing in their Sunday best. Helena was, as usual, making lunch for the fellowship. It was raining cats and dogs. Mr. Frederick went to Helena's house to pick her up and the treats she made.

When everyone arrived at church, they saw an unbelievable sight. In the middle of a circle, Turner stood in the pouring rain holding four cows. It was a miracle. The townspeople circled around him and began to pray. After they were finished praying, Ronnie and the others were eager to find out where Turner had been and where he got the cows.

All Turner would say were the words of Jesus: "Blessed are you who hunger and thirst, now you will be satisfied."

The women started singing praises to Jesus. The men called Turner a true hero.

Turner, in his soft, gentle voice, said, "Do not give glory to me; give the glory to God." The men looked at him with admiration in their eyes. At that moment, the rain stopped and a beautiful rainbow peeked through the clouds. No one seemed to mind they were soaked to the bone on a chilly November day.

Ronnie still wanted to question Turner, but his joy overtook his need to find out why. Turner then walked over to Ronnie and handed him the cows. Turner then said, "Brother Ronnie, you have given me friendship and a place to stay. You have made me your brother; now I give you these cows as a small token of my love."

Ronnie stood speechless. Instead of words, he just put his arms around Turner and wept. He then tied the cows to a post. The men joined the others inside the church.

Pastor Peter stood at his pulpit like he did so many times before, but today with a renewed spirit. He said, "This is the day the Lord has made. Let us rejoice and be glad."

All responded, "Amen." On that Sunday, their prayers of Thanksgiving were more heartfelt than ever before.

They were led by the pastor into the fellowship hall. In Thanksgiving of God's goodness, they would fast that Sunday and instead give all the treats to Sara. They wrapped a little wicker basket full of food and left a note inside of it. It read, "Sara, we all love you and our prayers are with you. Love your friends." Even Ruth was moved by the thoughtful people at the church.

Ronnie said, "We will take the basket to Sara on our way home."

Sister Victoria said. "I think it's better if Doc takes it to her." They all nodded in agreement.

Chapter 4

Sara sat near the window on the only chair she had that was not damaged in the fire. The cool fall air felt good on her hot skin. She looked around the three-room house. Inside she had very few belongings that were not destroyed. There was that red velvet chair she was sitting on that belonged to her father, a wash basin Doc gave her, a painted dish she ate off of that had belonged to her mother, two dresses, a quilt, and a hair comb. She thought to herself as she looked around the room, *God, why didn't you let me die. Even death would have been better than this existence I live now.* She was angry and bitter, and she hated all men, except for her father and Doc Benson. Her thoughts of depression were interrupted by Doc's secret knock he made up so she knew it was him.

Doc entered the room she was in. "Hello, my sweet Sara," he said. "I brought you something," he said.

"What is it?" she said flatly.

"Open it, and you will see." He couldn't see her eyes as she opened the gift because she wore a black veil over her face. The only time she took it off was when Doc examined her.

"I can't believe this. All this is for me? Take it back! I

don't deserve it. No one can ever love me this much." She carried much guilt and felt like a burden.

"No, it's for you Sara. We do love you, and you do deserve it." Doc reassured her.

Inside the basket were ham, fruit, cheese, tea, goat's milk, cookies, and penny candies. Under her veil, the Doc could hear her sobbing

"Doc, how can you love me? I look like a monster."

"My child, you are beautiful because you are God's daughter."

She denied that God could ever love her like this.

"Child, you eat something, and when you are ready, I will examine you."

Sara took her time eating because she hated the examination part of the visit with Doc. As Doc told her about the goings on in town, she stopped eating.

"You mean Turner Thomas? He was here a few weeks back nosing around Mama and Daddy's grave. I told him to take a hike. That Turner Thomas?" she said with a hint of Hope in her voice.

"Yes, that Turner Thomas," Doc said. Doc sat by, watching her eat. He noticed her swallowing was improving since the fire two years ago.

Sara said, "Okay, I guess I'm ready." She closed her eyes so she would not see Doc's expression as he lifted her veil. She had never seen it.

When Doc lifted the veil, he saw a beautiful creature of heaven. But she did not believe that. After the fire, she got rid of all her mirrors so she would never have to look at her own face again.

Her face was full of scar tissue and burnt skin. Her one eye was swollen shut. Doc said to her, "You are going to heal with God's help." He then put down her veil. He moved to her chest area. Her chest was not as bad as her face. Ronnie threw water on her to get the fire out. Doc then checked her arms, legs, and feet. Her nails that were once painted pastel colors were now blacker than night. Doc was pleased to see that no infection had set in since he removed her bandages a few months ago. Doc said to her, "I still wish you would travel with me to Paradise Gates to see if the doctors there can do a skin graph. Medicine is advancing, and it may—"

Before he could finish his thoughts, she answered with a poisonous no.

"But, Sara," Doc said.

"I said no. It's bad enough you have to see me like this. No one else will. Besides, even if they can do the surgery, do you think I deserve it after I drove my husband away?"

"Sara, my child, Larry was sick. He was a bad man, and you didn't drive him away." In his heart, he knew he would never win this argument. Sara's mind was too far gone to make her understand. He saw Sara was upset, so he quickly changed the subject to Morning Dew. Even though he could not see her face, he knew she was smiling. Morning Dew was her baby. Doc told her the latest news about her horse, how much he ate, how shiny his coat still was, and how he rode him proudly.

"Does he still like apples?" Sara asked. She then reached into the basket and found the shiniest, reddest apple. She said, "Please feed this to him." It took all of Doc's strength not to break down. In her own torment, she still had the kindest soul everyone remembered.

"Sara, I'm going to sit here until you fall asleep." Doc knew she was exhausted after the painful examination he given her.

"Okay," she said in a sleepy voice. It was not long after that she fell asleep.

Doc gingerly covered her up. He watched her sleep. He tiptoed across the bare wooden floor and slipped out the back door.

• • •

Mr. Frederick gazed at the beautiful new cows Turner brought home. He said gently to one of them, "Gonna milk now." He got a stool and his bucket. He milked the cows. He said to the wind, "More milk than Bess and other cows combined." He couldn't help but be overjoyed. Turner helped him today on the farm. He collected eggs and cleaned the stable and the pig Ronnie got hunting. He worked up a big appetite but there was something he had to do before he ate. He told Mr. Frederick he would be gone for a while.

• • •

When he arrived at Sara's doorstep, he found it hard to climb the stairs because the cement was crumbling so badly. He was very quiet as he left a tiny box at Sara's door. No one seemed to notice he was gone when he arrived at the breakfast table. He was happy about that. "Happy Thanksgiving," he said to the family. Everyone was in a cheery, bright mood. As they went around the table, each one thanked God for a blessing in their lives. When it came to Turner's turn, he chose to pray to himself.

"You really have outdone yourself this time, Mom," Little Ronnie said as he looked at the feast before him.

"This is only breakfast; just wait until supper," his mom said.

Turner to could not wait until dark because he knew then Sara would find her gift. On the Thanksgiving table, there were fresh cut flowers, mums, peonies, apple cider, fruit, jelly, bread, hotcakes, eggs, and oatmeal. Everyone was full.

Kim spent the rest of the morning preparing Thanksgiving dinner. She would be having a lot of guests tonight. Everyone in town, expect Sara and Ruth. Although the invitation stood, they would never come.

Pastor and Amy sat thinking about what they could do for Sara this Thanksgiving, for it was two years ago today that the fire happened. They knew Sara would not be all right today. They were very worried about her. They knew she would not eat today. So they didn't bring her food. Besides, she probably had more food left over from before.

"I know what we will do for Sara," Amy said excitedly. "We will ask Doc to bring Morning Dew over to see her. We will tell him to tell her that no one will be on Happiness Trail so if she wishes she can ride him."

"Darling, that is a great idea. I'm going to go to see the Doc now."

He went to Doc's office, but he was not there. He tried the general store. Anthony told him he was at the ice cream parlor.

Ruth was happy to get the business today. "May I help you?" she said.

"Yes, I'd like some ice cream to bring to the celebration. I will take some vanilla and chocolate."

Pastor told Doc about the idea. "It sounds great, but I doubt Sara will ride him."

"Have a little faith," Pastor said. "Don't be such

a doubting Thomas. Love can heal the most broken of hearts." Just then Ruth came back with the ice cream.

"How much?" Doc asked.

Ruth replied "Twenty-five cents."

He handed her a shiny new quarter. She put it in her drawer. "I'll see you tonight," she said, much to their surprise. "I need to talk to everyone tonight about Sara."

Doc looked her straight in the eye and said "What about Sara?"

"I'll talk to you tonight with everyone present," she answered.

Pastor rushed home to tell his wife about Ruth, Doc, and Morning Dew. Amy was worried about what Ruth had to say about Sara, but was excited about Doc bringing Sara's horse to see her.

Anna and Forest were very excited about the evening celebration. Anna was setting her hair with curlers. Forest came home from the lumber mill he worked at in the next town. "Do you like this dress I made it just for tonight?"

"I'm sure you will look stunning in it," Forest said.

"You better get washed so we won't be late," Anna said to her husband.

Anna looked like a movie star in her new dress. Her hair was curled and hung loose to her shoulders. In it was a blue comb her grandmother used to pull back her hair with. She was wearing light make up and painted her finger nails pink to match the dress she was wearing. Forest looked handsome in his suit.

Little Ronnie and Mr. Frederick went to pick up Sister Victoria and Helena so they wouldn't be alone in the dark. Mr. Frederick would have preferred to be alone with

Helena. Only if he could work up the nerve to court her properly. He was very shy.

Kim was in the kitchen putting last minute details on the dinner table. She was dressed in a delicate tan gown that she only wore on special occasions. Her hair was up in a bun. She was wearing pearl earrings and a pearl necklace.

Grandpa looked distinguished in his new suit. Ronnie looked dapper in his. Everyone would be arriving soon.

• • •

Sara always waited till dark to come out of the house. This evening was no different. When she cracked open the door to make sure no one was around, to her amazement she found Morning Dew grazing on the high grass in front of her house. She also saw a small box on her doorstep. For a moment, she was afraid this was some kind of trap. But she talked herself out of her fear and bent down to pick up the small box. She carried it inside. She sat down in the chair and examined it. *Should I open it? What do I have to lose?* When she opened it, she saw white tissue paper and a small note. She was not a good reader, but she knew some of the words. She made out the words *friends, love,* and *God.* Later on, she came to know what the letter truly stated. It read: "Dear Sara, you don't know me well yet, but I Hope to be your friend. God loves you. You are special to him. Love, your friend." As she pulled back the clean white paper, she found a pair of pink slippers, the kind she used to wear when she danced. They were her size. They had a pink satin ribbon running through it. For a fleeting moment, she felt happiness again as she remembered dancing freely. It brought joy to her face. She tried the slippers on, and they were a perfect fit. She looked up to the heavens and said, "God, do you really remember me?" Then she realized what day it was. She took the slippers off in a rage and threw them against the wall. Morning Dew, still outside, was grazing on the grass.

• • •

It was suppertime at the Miller farm. The first Miller guest to arrive was Anthony. He greeted them with a warm smile. He brought some penny candy for Kim in exchange for her warm hospitality. Next the pastor and his wife and then Old Doc, who brought ice cream. Then it was Anna and Forest. Soon after that, Little Ronnie, Mr. Frederick, Helena, and Sister. Then, to everyone's surprise, it was Ruth Brown.

Pastor said, "Please lead us in prayer."

Ronnie said, "Yes, of course." All bowed their heads. He prayed, "Heavenly Father, we thank thee for your bountiful gifts. We ask you to watch over Sara and us. We thank you for this day and our time together. Amen."

They lifted their heads. On the table was the prettiest feast anyone had ever seen. All the guests had name cards; the calligraphy writing looked like that of an artist. Each guest had a freshly cut flower at his or her place setting. There was hand-painted china, silver, and a silver teapot. In the middle of the table was a well-stuffed turkey. At the other end, the pig Ronnie caught. The pig was decorated with pineapples and cherries. The table was full of food. There was corn, carrots, greens, homemade bread, jam, sweet butter, cranberry dressing, cookies, cake, and pudding.

"Wow, this table is beautiful." Sister Victoria commented.

Everyone agreed. They ate, talked, sang, and gave thanks. Everyone was trying to pretend they were not bothered by the presence of Ruth. All of them wondered what she had to say about Sara.

After dinner, the women cleared the table and the men retired to the parlor. In the parlor, there was a piano and chairs for sitting. After the women cleaned the kitchen, they joined the men. Everyone toasted the expecting parents and guessed the sex of the baby. The room was filled with laughter.

Ruth cleared her throat. "Excuse me; it has taken me and all my courage to come here to share this. I hate to break up the party, but I have to tell you this."

All eyes were now on Ruth. The laughter that was in the room faded to a mere whisper. Ruth stood tall. She was a woman in his late sixties. She had an oval-shaped face. She always wore her hair tied in a bun. Her teeth were pearly white. Her dress was plain. She never wore make up or jewelry. As she stood in front of them, a hush fell over the room. She tried to read their faces, but they were as cold as stone.

"I don't know where to begin, so I'll just tell you the main facts. I have a younger sister." Everyone was amazed. She never spoke of family before. "She had a boy named Larry."

Sister Victoria dropped the cup she was drinking from. "You mean Larry? Larry Frank? You're his aunt?"

"I'm afraid so," she said shamefully.

"What? I don't believe it," Grandpa Miller said.

"Why didn't you say anything to us before?" Anna asked.

"If I would have told you that I was Larry's aunt, would you have accepted me? That's why I stayed away from you and never socialized with you. I carry so much blame, guilt, and shame. When Larry's mom abandoned him, I tried to be a mother figure to him, but I failed. I tried to stop him after the fire. I never heard from him again. I haven't heard from him—until recently, that is." She paused for a moment and then sobbed.

Ronnie's face turned from sympathy for the older woman to pure anger. "You get out of my house!" he shouted.

Turner, who was sitting quietly, got up and put his hand on Ron's shoulder. "Now brother, let us hear what she has to say."

Ronnie grew calmer. Helena turned white as a ghost. She and Sara grew up together. The pain was too much. She passed out. Doc ran to her side. He put wet clothes on her forehead. When she woke up, Doc held her tightly in his arms like she was a baby. Mr. Frederick watched helplessly as the woman he loved heart shattered into a million pieces. Pastor tried to calm the helpless situation with prayer. Amy and Sister clung to each other. Little Ronnie and Joseph were barely able to breathe.

Turner, in a low, gentle tone, said, "We must listen to what she has to say."

Forest interrupted him. "I'm sorry, Turner. My wife is with child; she can't get upset like this."

Everyone agreed. It was best they went home.

Inside everyone was growing angrier with Ruth. Pastor and Turner worked hard to keep harmony in the room. Ruth could hardly allow the words to come from her mouth.

"Sara does not know, nor has she ever known, that I am Larry's aunt. After the two got married, Larry contacted me. I was afraid of Larry's growing temper. I found them here and settled in for a new life in Summerville Heights when rumors started rising of Larry's troubled mind. I was secretly meeting him to try to steer him back to Christ. One time I even took him to see a doctor in Gingerbread Landing to try to help him with his problems. Just about two weeks ago, I got a letter from Larry." Her voice was hoarse; her eyes were full of tears. "I need to read this to you so you will understand."

How much could this small town take? How much longer could this community of friends be strong?

With shaky hands she pulled the letter from her dress pocket. It looked like she had read it a million times. With an unsteady voice, she read it to them. "My dearest Aunt Ruth, a lot of hours and days have passed since the night of that fire. After the fire, my conscience haunted me. I tried to out run it but failed. I was plagued with nightmares of Sara's screams. I ran but couldn't get away from what I did. My soul does not deserve mercy or forgiveness. I am evil. I have spent the last two years rotting away behind steel bars. I do not seek pity. Words cannot express how sorry I am to you, Sara, and the town. I Hope Sara can find some comfort in knowing I turned myself in and I am suffering greatly, but not with only my loss of freedom but my health too. I will spend my last days seeking forgiveness from God. I Hope this letter will bring you peace in knowing nothing was your fault. You cannot control the evil inside me. I myself cannot control it. I just want everyone to know the monster you know me as died when he was caged like a wild animal. I deserve all the unhappiness I get. You deserve joy and happiness. I will not contact you again, and do not try to contact me. For when you receive this letter, I will have entered into my eternal damnation. I'm sorry. Larry."

No one could speak or move. They could hardly blink. Slowly they came out of their shock. Turner was the first to speak. "I think we need to pray for God to give us the wisdom to know what to do."

Mr. Frederick, the shy man who did not read or write, took everyone by surprise when he offered a heartfelt prayer. "Father, we come to you as brothers and sisters. Please help us find the healing we seek; help us to find forgiveness in our hearts for this man."

It was like God was speaking through this shy immigrant. Helena found compassion in her heart. She found the strength to look past her pain and see Ruth's. She pulled herself off the floor, walked over to Ruth, and embraced her. There was a hint of vulnerability in Ruth's eyes no one had ever seen before. Her voice was filled with gratitude as she said thank you.

Pastor said, "We can't focus on the past right now. We have to focus on Sara. I do believe that sharing this letter with her or that Ruth is Larry's aunt will do Sara more harm than good. What do you think, Doc? You know Sara best."

Doc pondered the question for a while. Then he said, "I think so, but I do want to travel into the Hidden Valley tomorrow and see if Larry is really sick or trying to scheme us."

Ronnie and Frederick said, "We will go with you." Ruth remained silent as the men talked about this.

Then she said, "I sure Hope he found some peace and went to God so he may find peace too."

The long night ended with the three men agreeing to go see Larry. Everyone promised not to tell Sara. Ruth won over their forgiveness.

Chapter 5

Sara slept almost peacefully that night. A nightmare awoke her once, but she drifted back to sleep right away. On most nights, Sara would awake to her own terrifying screams. Sara woke in the morning feeling hungry. She ate some jam and bread. She then poured some water in the washbasin and washed herself. As she slipped on a clean dress, she remembered the kind stranger's gift. At first she thought she was dreaming, but as she adjusted her eyes to the sunlight from her sleepy state, she saw the slippers were still against the wall where she threw them the night before. She wondered if her horse was still grazing on high grass in her yard. But she would never take the chance of allowing someone to see her in the daylight. She walked over to the slippers and touched them, almost afraid to hold them. She fought her fear back down deep into her gut. She slipped the slippers on, and she began to dance. She felt alive again. She daydreamed that she was performing with a famous ballet company. A smile came upon her face. She spent the rest of the morning dancing.

• • •

Forest caught up with Ronnie that morning. Ronnie filled him in on what happened after he left that night.

"How is Ann? " Ronnie asked.

"Okay now, but she spent half the night crying. You know I would go with you if I could."

Old Doc was already at the Miller farm. He too had arrived early that morning. Mr. Frederick was gathering up what supplies they would need for their journey. Kim, Turner, and Little Ronnie were helping him. Grandpa was getting the horses and wagon ready.

Turner said to Ronnie, "I sure wish you would let me come."

"I need someone here to look after the family and the farm. So it's best you stay here," Ronnie replied.

"The nights are getting colder, and I've taught you how to run the farm." Just then, Grandpa came from the stable. "The horses and wagon are ready," he announced.

Kim did not want to let go of her husband as she kissed him goodbye. She said, "I've packed plenty of food and warm clothes for your journey."

Turner suggested they pray for the men; so they took each other's hands. It was Little Ronnie who said this prayer: "Psalms 61: 'Here my cry, oh Lord; listen to my prayer. From the ends of the earth I call to you, I call as my heart grows faint; lead me to the rock that is higher than I. For you are my refuge, a strong tower against my foe."

Ronnie was proud of his son. He knew at that moment his son was no longer a boy but a man. All wished the men strength from God as they traveled. It would take three days to arrive, but there were many dangers along the way. Forest left to get back to Anna. Standing alone there was Turner, Grandpa, Little Ronnie, and Kim.

Pastor Peter looked at his pocket watch. He said to Amy, "They must be leaving the farm now." Pastor and

Amy knelt at the altar of their church and prayed for the men.

Just at the same hour, Sister Victoria, Anthony, and Helena gathered to pray.

Ruth although forgiven by her neighbors, prayed alone in her ice cream parlor.

• • •

As the men passed Sara's house, they wondered what she was doing. As they traveled down Happiness Trail, they discussed what they would say when they saw Larry face-to-face. Old Doc, being admired in the group, was looking toward for having the answers. He did not know himself. He shared that honestly with Ronnie and Mr. Frederick. They sat silently for a while. When then got to the end of Happiness Trail, they knew the rough road would begin.

At the end of Happiness Trail, they decided to pull over and have some lunch. They also wanted to give Freedom and Liberty a rest. Kim had packed for them ham sandwiches, coleslaw, sweet tea, coffee, beans, and corn. They ate some of the ham sandwiches.

Ronnie then said, "We will be reaching the dirt road that will be leading to Gingerbread Landing soon."

Mr. Frederick knew the backwoods like the back of his hand. He knew there would be many dangers ahead. There was a very heavily wooded area where no light ever shined through the trees. In those woods would be snakes of the poisonous kinds, queen beehives, wild boar, and the shack people who did not like strangers.

Ronnie offered a prayer before they entered those woods. They also decided to sleep in four-hour shifts so someone would always be awake to look for any dangers that could befall them. Ronnie took out his shotgun and said, "I'll take the first shift."

• • •

Kim paced the floor of her parlor, nearly wearing a hole in it. It had been nearly two days now since her husband, Old Doc, and Mr. Frederick left for their journey. Turner, Grandpa, and Little Ronnie were taking very good care of the farm. They were very anxious to hear from the other men.

Kim busied her mind with making a dress for Sara and a hat as a very special Christmas present. Anna, Sister Victoria, Ruth, Helena, and Amy came to keep her company every day until her husband returned.

Pastor Peter, Forest, and Anthony took care of Doc's office while he was gone.

Turner also continued to leave small gifts for Sara. He even got the men that were left behind to clean up her yard and rebuild her steps.

Sara still would not appear to any of them, but Turner was winning her trust. One night he even thought he saw Sara riding Morning Dew, but he could not say for certain.

On Sunday they gathered for church service. They prayed for the men and their safe return. They did not hold fellowship.

• • •

The trees were bare, and the fall wind had turned into newly fallen snow. The men made it through Gingerbread Landing safely and were very close to Shady Woods. The men were tired and cold. They were down to the last bit of food Kim had packed. When they saw a small hand-painted wooden sign that said shady woods" they rejoiced in the beautiful sights of that sign.

Ronnie said, "I think before we enter shady woods we should say a prayer"

Mr. Frederick and Old Doc agreed that was a good idea. As Old Doc prayed, it almost seemed like Freedom and Liberty were bowing their heads too. After the men finished praying, they continued on to shady woods men had heard of this place all their lives but never dared to enter. Grandpa Miller had told Ronnie and Mr. Frederick once of the violent and sinful men that would hide there from their dirty crimes. Old Doc once treated a man that rode through Summerville Heights from there half beaten.as they entered. The trees were covered with snow. The leaves that had fallen from the trees now hid the grass that was probably as green as emerald grass in Ireland.

There was no church in sight. Down a narrow dirt road, they entered into the valley square. They could not see any signs of life at all. There was not even a deer in sight. It sent cold shivers down the men's spines. In the square, they noticed a two-story boarding house that looked like no one had stayed in for a while. There was a little stable, but it had no horses. And there was a house that they could see ladies of the night lived in. This was an ungodly town for sure.

Ronnie said, "I think we should turn back now; this place is giving me an awfully bad feeling."

Old Doc said, "Me too, but if we don't continue on our mission, we will never know if Larry was lying to us or not."

Mr. Frederick remained quiet as the two men talked.

Old Doc convinced Ronnie that they must go on. Just as they passed a little house, they saw one of the ladies of the night walk their way. "You boys looking, or do you have a woman in mind already?"

Old Doc responded, "Neither, but we are looking for the jail."

"Are you turning yourselves in, or are you looking for someone there?"

Old Doc's impatience with her was growing quite evident. "Can you tell us where the jail is or not? Enough of these disgusting questions. Do you know how to get to the jail?" he asked.

The lady seemed to bask in his take-charge attitude. "Okay, I'll tell you. You go down the dirt road behind the stable. You will find the law there, but if you change your mind about the girls, you will know where to find me."

None of the men thanked her and pulled away before she could say anything else.

They steered Liberty and Freedom toward the dirt road. They followed it all the way to the end. There they found the jail. Nervously, they entered the big iron doors. In front of them was a long desk. Sitting behind it was the town sheriff.

"You don't look like you belong here," he said. The man in his thirties was very muscular. He looked like he could handle himself and defend himself very well. He was wearing a brown-colored uniform; around his waist were two guns.

Ronnie nervously explained why they were there.

"I'm sorry," the sheriff said in a very compassionate voice. "If you want to talk to Larry face-to-face, you are too late. He passed away Thanksgiving evening. We buried him out in Potters Field." The man went on to say that Larry was very remorseful for what he did. He spent his last days seeking forgiveness from his maker.

Old Doc suddenly felt very sorry for the man they came to know as Larry the monster. So he asked the other men to join him to pray for the lost soul. The other men did as he requested.

Then the tall sheriff offered them a place to stay for the evening. The sheriff offered them a room in his old stable where they would be safe and warm. The men stayed there that night. In the morning, the sheriff's wife packed them hot cakes, milk, fruit, and turkey to take back on the journey home. The men headed home early in the morning.

• • •

"Momma, Momma, come quick!" Little Ronnie said. His mother came rushing out of the kitchen where she was preparing food.

"Anthony is here to take you to see Anna. She has gone into labor," Little Ronnie explained.

Kim grabbed her herbs that she could use to help Anna with her labor pains. Anthony and Kim rushed over to Forest and Anna's small three-room cottage. The cottage was just a little ways down Happiness Trail. Surrounding the cottage, there were crape maple trees, a fruit orchard, and a small wooden fence. When Anthony and Kim arrived at the cottage, they could see Old Faithful grazing outside.

"Good, at least Sister Victoria is already here with Anna, "Kim said.

When they walked inside the little brown cottage

made of scrap wood that Forest had gotten from the lumberyard, they saw that Sister Victoria had things under control. Anna was lying on her feather bed, her head and back propped up with pillows.

"Hello, Anna. Dear, how are you feeling?" Kim asked.

Anna's face gave her the only answer she needed. It was twisted from labor pains.

"Here, I'll fix some of these herbs I brought to help you with that," Kim said. Anna managed to give her half a smile. "Where is Forest?" Kim asked.

"He is at the lumber mill. Pastor went to get him," Sister Victoria answered. Just then there was a knock at the door.

It was Amy, Helena, and Ruth. They all came to help with the birth. They were worried with Old Doc being out of town.

"You need not worry. Back in my younger days I was a midwife, "Sister Victoria explained. They were all relieved by her comment.

Anthony Joseph waited outside the cottage; he attended to the horses. There was Candy Apple, Ruth's horse; Old Faithful; Little Friend; and Big Bear, Forest's horse. He gave them fresh hay and cleaned the stable. He knew Forest would have his hands full when he got home from the mill.

The labor pains were sharper now and coming closer together. Helena held a wet cloth to Anna's head. Amy held her hand. Ruth started preparing food for after the birth. Kim was reading Scriptures from the Bible.

Sister Victoria whispered to Kim, "This is going to be a long, hard birth for Anna. It's going to be a long night."

Anna screamed with a sharp intense pain. Forest

finally arrived home. He did what he could to help Anna through the labor.

Turner, Grandpa, and Little Ronnie were back at the farm waiting for any news about Ronnie, Old Doc, and Mr. Frederick. Late afternoon turned into early evening. There was no news about the men or Anna.

The night fell upon Summerville Heights. "Push, Anna, push," Sister Victoria said in a smooth, gentle voice.

"The baby is almost here," Helena said, excited.

With one final push, Anna heard the cry of her baby.

"It's a boy," Sister Victoria said with a strong, proud voice.

"Let me wash him a little before I hand him to you," Ruth said.

Anna said, sobbing, "Is he healthy?"

"Sure sounds like a healthy cry to me," Amy said.

Sister and Ruth washed the baby. Then they handed him to Anna.

• • •

From the outside where the men were waiting in the stables, they could hear the cries of the newborn. Helena pushed the big stable door open. The smile she was wearing stretched from ear to ear.

"Well, Forest, are you going to stay out in the stables all night with the horses, or are you going to introduce yourself to your son?"

The men let out a cheer that sounded like the thunder in the heavens. They all embraced Forest. Pastor let them in prayer before they went in to see Anna.

Inside, Anna was cradling their new son. She held

him close to her breast and rocked him. Forest ran to his wife and kissed her.

"He has your eyes ... beautiful, precious eyes," he said.

"Well he got your nose," she said. They both started laughing. Then the emotion of the day both caught up with them.

Sister saw that the new mamma, daddy, and baby needed time alone, so she said, "There's much time for celebrating; right now Anna and the baby need their rest." With that, every one said a prayer and went home.

"I'll take you home, Kim. I'm anxious to see if the men have returned with any news of Larry," Ruth said. Kim could understand that even though Larry had made some awful mistakes, Ruth was still his aunt and deep down inside still held love for him.

• • •

It was nighttime, Sara's mask for being able to move about freely outside without being seen. She estimated the time between being somewhere about midnight. Sara wanted to touch the cold, freezing, newly fallen snow. It always made her remember days when her parents were still alive. They used to have snowball fights, build snowmen, and go sleigh-riding. She could not stay outside long, though, because she did not have a pair of gloves or a good winter coat. She longed for the day her parents were alive. Long before the horrible fire destroyed her life. She peered outside the door. She heard the sound of a horse coming up Happiness Trail. *Who would be out this late?* She would have to wait for Doc to come by to see her. He would certainly have the answer.

When Doc came to visit, he always told her about

what was going on with her friends in town. She wished she had a candle to light; at least then she could put her slippers on and dance. Sara spent most of the daytime sleeping. She cursed the sunlight. Only on days Doc came by was she a little happier. Sara fumbled around in the dark to find the slippers the kind stranger had given her. She held them close to her heart. Then, for the first time in ages, she felt like God still cared. So she whispered, "God, if you're listening, let me someday meet this kind stranger so I may thank him in person." Sara fell back into a deep sleep, holding the slippers near her heart.

• • •

Kim and Ruth returned to the Miller farm. They were ecstatic to see that the men had returned home safely. They both got off of Candy Apple. Ruth quickly patted Candy Apple down before she went inside. Kim did not wait till she was finished. She was anxious to see her husband and hold him.

Little Ronnie was already asleep, so they did not wake him. Turner, Grandpa, Old Doc, and Mr. Frederick were sitting in the parlor drinking coffee. They had a high fire built in the fireplace. Kim ran over to her husband and embraced him.

"I've missed you so much," she said.

Then she embraced Old Doc and Mr. Frederick.

Ruth came into the parlor. She stood in the doorway because she did not want to interrupt this tender moment.

"Come in please; sit down. We need to talk to you," Ronnie invited.

From the tone of his voice, she could already tell what

the men had to say. She started sobbing immediately. Turner put his arm around her to comfort her. "Where have they buried him?" she asked.

"Before we discuss that, we need to tell you something," Old Doc said.

"Please don't tell me if it is unbearable. Larry was all I had left of my family, and although he did unspeakable things, I loved him. He was my kin." Her weeping was even harder now.

"What we are about to tell you may bring you some peace," Mr. Frederick said.

Ronnie explained. "When we went to see the law and we spoke to him about Larry, the sheriff said that Larry was truly remorseful for what he did and he spent his last days seeking forgiveness from God. The sheriff said he made peace with his maker."

This seemed to bring Ruth comfort, as well as Kim. Ruth stopped crying. In a heartfelt gesture, Kim and Ronnie looked at each other. They were almost able to read each other's minds. Ronnie said, "Ruth, we have forgiven you and Larry, and I think most of the townspeople will too after they hear how sorry Larry was. You do have family. We're your family now."

Ruth almost collapsed; her knees were shaky. "Oh, thank you! Thank you for your forgiveness, kindness, and love." They hugged. "Now please tell me where they laid Larry so I may give him a proper burial and maybe someday bring him home."

Mr. Frederick then told her where Larry was resting.

Turner then led them in prayer. "Heavenly Father, you sent your Son Jesus to earth to teach us to love and forgive. Even on the cross your Son forgave those who sinned against him. Thank you, Jesus, for forgiving Larry. Thank you for giving us the gift of neighbors and family. Lord, please let Larry have a peaceful eternal rest in your kingdom, and please heal Sara's body, mind, soul, and spirit. Amen."

Just then, Little Ronnie heard the voices of his father, Mr. Frederick, and Old Doc. He jumped out of bed to greet them. His father told him about their journey and Larry. With overwhelming compassion in his Christian heart, he turned to Ruth. "You will be my aunt now."

Ruth hugged him so tight he almost couldn't breathe. Everyone in the room started crying and couldn't stop.

Then Kim turned to Ronnie, Old Doc, and Mr. Frederick, and said, "There's a new stranger in town!" The men looked at her very confused while the others were laughing. "Little Ronnie, you better get that list of baby boy names ready because Anna and Forest will need them tomorrow."

"You mean Anna had the baby?" Old Doc asked.

"Yes, she sure did, a healthy baby boy. Ten fingers, ten toes, a little butter ball," Ruth said. Suddenly the sadness turned into joy.

Turner reminded them what was written in Scripture in Ecclesiastes 3. "There is a time for everything and a season for every activity under heaven: a time to be born and a time to die, a time to plant and a time to uproot, a time to kill and a time to heal, a time to weep and a time to laugh, a time to mourn and a time to dance."

Suddenly everything became crystal clear to them. God took Larry so a new baby could be born. It was so late, everyone was tried. They all slept peacefully.

"Rock-a-bye baby." Anna sat in the rocking chair that

Forest made as a special gift for her and the baby. "Your first sunrise," she said as she looked out the window of her bedroom. It had been the first time she watched the sun awaken in ages.

"Sweetheart, are you still up?" Forest said thoughtfully to his wife.

"I just woke up a little while ago. I had to feed the baby," she replied.

Forest said, "I want to hold my son." He was smiling.

"Okay, Papa Bear, just be careful with his head." Just like a worrying mom would say, Anna gently handed baby over to Forest. She climbed back into bed. Almost immediately after her head hit the pillows, she was fast asleep.

"I can't wait till Little Ronnie gives me the list of baby names for you. We have to get you named soon," Forest said, looking down proudly at his son. He rocked back and forth, holding the tiny baby that was wrapped in a blue blanket. He had dark eyes and dimples. He had only one little strand of brown hair on his head. Forest talked to his son for hours, telling him how he would one day show him how to make furniture like the rocking chair, telling him his Hopes and dreams for his son. He then woke Anna up to feed the baby. While Anna was feeding the baby, Forest surprised his wife with lunch in bed.

• • •

Amy was planning a surprise party for Anna, Forest, and baby. She took Heaven's Light to the general store to pick up some things she would need for the party. Anthony was still beaming from ear to ear that Anna gave birth to a boy. He was the only one in town that thought she was going to have a boy. Amy and Anthony made small talk.

Then Anthony said, "I've got in this fine lace material; it would be the perfect material for the baby's christening suit." Anthony gave it to Amy at no charge. It was his gift to the baby.

Just then Doc came into the store. Everyone was glad to see him back. They knew it was a rough journey. Doc told Anthony and Amy about what happened on the trip.

"How is Ruth holding up?" Amy asked. Doc told her. Amy said she was going to go check on her. She needed the support right now. No one in town blamed her for what happened.

"I'm going over now to check on Anna and then on Sara," Old Doc said.

"If you're going over to Sara's, I have something new for her. I'll be right back with it." Anthony disappeared into a back storeroom. Amy and Doc discussed the party that would take place after the christening on Sunday.

"It will just be what we need to start healing. I just wish Sara could be there," Old Doc said.

"Me too," Amy replied.

"I think this is Sara's size," Anthony said. In his hand he was holding a beautiful pair of velvet red gloves and a coat to match.

"Where in the world did you get something so beautiful?" Amy asked.

"Last year, I made a deal with the general store in Paradise Gates that if I sent them $2.00 a week, they would hold this for me until this winter. It took me a whole year to pay for it, but this year Sara is going to have the coat and gloves she deserves," Anthony said.

They were very touched by his gift. "You are a true

testament of what love can do. I just wish you could see Sara's face when I give it to her," Doc said to Anthony.

"I might not be able to see her face, but I will feel her happiness in my heart," Anthony replied.

"I'm going to go see Ruth now. I'll see you on Sunday," Amy said. She then said goodbye to her friends.

• • •

Turner had another idea to show Christ's love to Sara. He would talk to the townsfolk about it Sunday afternoon. Kim was busy working on a gift for Sara that she wanted to finish by Christmas. She sat at her Singer sewing machine working on the dress for Sara. If she had any extra material, she was going to make a handbag to match it.

Turner wanted to have a heart-to-heart talk with Mr. Frederick about Helena. He went outside to where Mr. Frederick was collecting eggs from the chicken coup. "Mr. Frederick, do you have a moment. I'd like to talk with you."

"I have many moments for you, friend," Mr. Frederick replied.

"I want to talk to you about Helena."

Mr. Frederick had a panicked look on his face. "You're not sweet on my Helena, are you?" he said in a matter-of-fact tone.

"No, that's not it at all. Not at all. I noticed you call her 'my Helena.' Do you love her?" Turner asked. Mr. Frederick's face turned blush red.

"Are you my friend? You won't laugh, right?" Mr. Frederick questioned Turner.

"We are brothers. I would never laugh at you. Is there anything I could do to help you?"

"I love Helena, but I'm not good enough for her," Mr. Frederick added.

"Not good enough? You are the most honorable man I know. You deserve happiness, and so does Helena. If you love each other, you should be together."

"But I not read, write, or talk good English. Helena deserve better," Mr. Frederick said sadly.

"Frederick, is that all that's holding you back from courting Helena?" Turner listened very attentively while Mr. Frederick told him about his past. He was married and had children. Their house was burned down during a civil war in Krakow, Poland. "Wouldn't your wife want you to be happy?"

"Yes, yes, but that's not holding me back from loving Helena. How can I give good life for her if I cannot read, write, or know good English?"

Turner said, "Brother, if I taught you these things, would you then court Helena?"

"Yes, yes," Mr. Frederick said gratefully.

"Then every night we will meet here secretly in the stable, and I will teach you. You are my brother. I want to help your dreams come true."

• • •

It was nearly noon when Old Doc arrived at Anna's house. The new mom was sitting in her kitchen, holding her baby, and stirring goat's milk. Little Ronnie and Ronnie had come by earlier with the list of baby names. Before they left, Anna, Forest, and Little Ronnie had decided on the name John Michael. Old Doc was thrilled to see John Michael. He was even more thrilled to see that mommy and baby were fine and healthy. Old Doc told them about Anthony's gift to Sara. They were very moved.

"Old Doc, we have a gift for Sara too. Some of the men at the lumber mill were very moved to hear about the newest details in Sara's journey, so they made this for her." It was a jewelry box. It was carved out of mahogany wood and stained with the finest stain. Inside of it was a beautiful pair of earrings and some fancy powder.

"Sara will be overjoyed with all the gifts I will be bringing her today. If I'm going to get to her house, I better get going. I will come by in a few days to check on you. Congratulations again," Old Doc said.

Forest walked Old Doc out. He wanted to talk to him alone. "Doc, I have a question about John Michael. I was embarrassed to ask in front of Anna. Is it normal for the baby to have a rash on his bottom?"

Doc almost let out a chuckle, but he didn't want to insult Forest. "Yes, very normal." He then explained what the rash was.

"Thanks, Doc. I feel so much better," Forest said.

As Doc got on Healer, he said, "If you and Anna have any more questions, don't be afraid to ask." Then Doc and Healer were out of sight.

• • •

Sara sat at the window trying to peek out without being seen. She thought to herself, *I guess Doc is not coming today. I really wanted to show him my slippers.* She was heartbroken. Doc was her only link to the outside world. She really wanted to know who was riding that horse so late the other night. She looked around at her pitiful house. She was overcome by its sight in the full sunlight and began to cry. Once again, she was wondering if God was listening. So, in a desperate attempt to find out, she prayed this prayer: "God, if you care about me, if you still love me, please send Old Doc today." To her amazement, as soon as she finished breathing that prayer, she heard Old Doc's secret knock!

She was taken back. She did not answer right away. So he knocked again. Old Doc entered the house with the surprise gifts hidden in his medicine satchel so Sara would not see them right away. "Hello, my sweet Sara; how are you feeling today?"

To his surprise, Sara said, "A little better."

Every time he would come to see her, her answer to that question would be "How would you feel if you looked like a strange creature?" Doc filled her in on the happenings around town. She took great interest in new baby John Michael. She secretly wished she could hold him and see him. "Did you eat today?" Doc asked her.

"Well the basket is getting low, so I wanted to save what I had left for supper."

"We figured that, so we put together a new one for you. Inside the basket are deer meat, coffee, eggs, and a pumpkin pie."

"Thank you," Sara said.

"Now you eat; then I'll examine you, and then I have yet another surprise." Old Doc said.

"I have a surprise for you too," Sara said.

What could it be? Had Sara changed her mind about the surgery?

Sara fixed some deer meat and coffee. "Did you eat, Doc?" she said. It almost seemed like a hint of the old Sara.

"Yes, I ate by Anna and Forest's house," Doc replied. She ate, and then Doc examined her.

"You first," Sara said of the surprise.

Old Doc carefully pulled out the jewelry box the men at the mill made. "Oh, my God, it's so beautiful!" Sara cried.

"Open it," Doc said.

Sara lightly lifted the lid of the delicate jewelry box. "Oh, my God! Oh, my God! It's just like the one Mamma and Daddy gave me on my sweet sixteen."

"Yes, Sara, I remember."

"Oh, my God," she said as her heart raced with excitement.

"There's something else too," Old Doc said softly. "This is from Anthony; he says, 'Merry Christmas' early."

Sara could no longer hide the fact that she was crying. She looked at the velvet gloves and velvet coat. No man had ever given her a gift like that except for the slippers.

"Try them on, Sara," Old Doc said.

Sara's hand was so shaky she needed Doc's help trying them on. "You look so beautiful, my sweet Sara." The soft velvet against her skin made her remember when her skin was soft and creamy. Next Sara tried on the coat. It was too big for her, but Sara didn't mind. The warm velvet and fur collar reminded her of the days she used to bask in the summer sun.

Doc could see the beautiful Sara smiling like she used to.

"Now, Doc, it's my turn to give you your surprise." She first told him the story of how she got the slippers. Then she asked him to read the note that came with them. She memorized the words by heart. Sara then put the slippers on and danced! She danced and danced. Doc was too moved to speak. He just sat there and watched Sara dance. As she was dancing, her veil slipped off and the harsh reality of her past came to light. She could not see that Doc did not look at her face in horror. He only looked with joy.

"Get out. You take these things and get out!" she screamed. She took off the slippers, gloves, and coat. "These things will never make me beautiful again!"

Doc tried to calm her down. After a while, he finally got her calm. He was then able to talk to her. "Sara, my sweet and lovely Sara, don't you know that the body is only the outer shell for the spirit inside? God doesn't judge us by our looks but by our hearts. He loves you, Sara, and the people of Summerville Heights. We will never abandon you, make fun of you, or hurt you," Doc said.

This was the first time Sara was listening, really listening, to his words since the fire. "Sara, Larry was a bad man, but I know he is sorry for what he did."

At the name of Larry, Sara began to cry. "Why did he do it, Doc? Why? I loved him."

"Because he was sick, sweetie. Because he was hurting too."

Sara reached out for Doc's arm for the first time ever. Doc took her and held her. "Sara, I love you," Doc said.

"I love you too, Doc," Sara said.

"Take off your veil and look at me. I won't laugh. I promise, Sara. I won't be horrified," Doc said.

"I … I … I can't."

"Sara, you have been living in darkness too long. Take off the veil, and let the light be on your face," Doc said.

"I'm afraid. I'm afraid you will run away and I'll be alone forever." Sara cried. Slowly, Sara removed her veil and looked into Doc's eyes since before the fire. The warmth in his eyes told her she would never be alone. "I'm sorry for getting mad at you. Promise me you won't tell anyone about this night, about seeing me without my veil."

Sara and Doc both cried. This was a real breakthrough for Sara. Sara was not ready for surgery yet, but she now was one step closer.

•   •   •

Turner excused himself from the dinner table. "I'm going outside for a breath of fresh air."

"You will freeze out there. If you're going to insist on going out, take my warmest coat," Ronnie said.

"Thank you," Turner said. Turner did not tell them he was just going to the stables to give Mr. Frederick his first lesson in reading and writing.

Mr. Frederick waited excitedly in the stable for Turner. By the flicker of two small lanterns, they sat on a stack of hay. "Now, Mr. Frederick, the first lesson I will teach you is your ABCs."

•   •   •

Helena was working on a special gift to give Sara for Christmas. She sat by her fireplace with her sewing needle. With every stitch, there was love. Growing up, Sara and Helena loved to have tea parties and play dress up. The gift Helena was making was a lace tablecloth; she was also making her a new blanket. *She will love this,* she thought to herself. As she sat by the fire, childhood memories of her and Sara came rushing through her mind. She could almost see childhood dreams in the embers of the fire. Helena knew that someday she would get her childhood friend back. She never gave up Hope. She finished sewing the tablecloth. She then whispered a prayer to God for Sara.

• • •

Pastor Peter and Amy were going over last minute details about the christening. Neither could wait. Both of them thought about how a new baby brings Hope and new dreams. Pastor Peter looked outside the window of his church. "It is snowing again," he said.

"I sure Hope it does not snow too hard. Anna will never be able to bring the baby out in it like that," Amy said.

Sister Victoria was the first one to arrive at church that Sunday. She was dressed in a long wool dress, a heavy coat, and gloves.

"Sure is cold out," she said.

"Very unusual for Georgia," Pastor replied back.

Sister Victoria had a special gift for John Michael: a pretty blue baby rattle. "I've had this in my Hope chest since I was a little girl," she revealed.

Amy Carrie said, "I'm sure John will love it." Sister took her seat.

The next one to arrive at church was Anthony. Anthony was dressed in a dark blue suit. His hair was white from snow falling on it. He greeted the pastor and his wife. He then showed them the gift he had for baby John. It was the cutest pair of leather shoes. "Sure Hope they fit," he said.

"I'm sure they will," Pastor said. Anthony took a seat next to Victoria.

The Miller family pulled up in front of their church with their wagon. They threw wool blankets over Liberty and Freedom because the snow was really falling down. Turner helped Grandpa down off the wagon. Ronnie helped Kim. They were all dressed so nice. Little Ronnie had two very special gifts for the baby: a book called *The Three Bears* and a blanket he made out of bearskin to keep the baby warm. Turner was going to give John Michael his most treasured possession: his aunt's Bible. He hoped that it would give John as much happiness as it had given him. His gift was thoughtful and unselfish. Ruth, Helena, and Old Doc came to the church together.

Finally Anna, Forest, and John. Anna looked like a princess in her new silk brown dress that Kim had given her for this occasion. Forest looked handsome in his brown suit and tie. John Michael looked like a little angel in his crisp, pure-white suit that the pastor's wife had made.

"This is the day the Lord has made; let us rejoice and be glad," Pastor said from his pulpit. Everyone shouted amen. There was pure electricity in the church. You could feel the Spirit of God fall upon them. Pastor continued. "He took a little child and had him stand among them. Taking him in his arms, he said to them, 'Whoever welcomes one of these children in my name welcomes me.' Mark 9:36." Pastor then took baby John and poured water all over his head and said, "I baptize you in the name of the Father, Son, and Holy Spirit." A look of joy beamed in John's little face.

A hush fell upon the church when Ruth got up and said, "Pastor, will you baptize me too so I may give my live to Christ and will only walk with him from this moment on?"

Pastor, with tears in his eyes, said, "Yes, my child, but who would be your Godparents?"

Victoria and Anthony both stood up and said, "We will."

So they walked up to the altar, Sister on the right side of Ruth, Anthony on the left. Pastor then poured out water over Ruth's head and said, "Your sins are forgiven. I baptize you in the name of our Lord, Jesus Christ." It was a miracle. Everyone cried.

After the baptism, everyone walked over to the fellowship hall. Helena and Amy had made mouth-watering food. The hall was all decorated too. Anthony had supplied all the decorations. There was blue and white crepe paper all around. There was a beautiful shimmering silver cross, and on all the tables, there was lace tablecloth and blue flowers. Everyone was in awe of how beautiful the hall looked. Pastor blessed the food, and they ate. Everyone talked about how beautiful the day was; they were all in happy spirits.

After they ate Turner talked to everyone about the gift he would like to give Sara for Christmas. They all agreed it would be just what Sara needed.

It was three weeks before Christmas. Everyone was working feverishly to get the surprise done for Sara. The little town square was all decorated. Around all the light posts in town, Anthony tied red bows. In the middle of the town square, Forest made a small manger. Old Doc had a small evergreen in his office decorated with string popcorn and penny candies. Ruth had a pretty wreath hanging on the door of her ice cream parlor. Inside she had a stuffed Santa Claus doll. Victoria made a small doll for John Michael; it was an elf doll. The Miller family decorated their wagon with red ribbon and evergreen. Helena was busy making pies. She made apple, cranberry, cherry, and pumpkin.

"It is finished," Kim said excitedly to Grandpa. "It's beautiful. Sara will look great in it." Kim proudly held up the dress she made for Sara. It was a flowing beautiful gown made of lace. It was of green color. It had a white satin ribbon going through the waist. Kim also had enough material to make a pocketbook and hat. The pocketbook had white trim, so did the hat.

• • •

Turner and Mr. Frederick went out in the stable doing their nightly lessons. Mr. Frederick would be ready soon to court Helena properly. He had learned so much in a short time. He now knew how to spell and write his name, his ABCs, and last week he read his first book. His English was getting better too. Turner told him how proud he was of him and all his accomplishments.

• • •

"Look, look! Baby John is sitting up, Papa Bear," Anna tenderly said. Forest was so excited.

"Mama Bear, he's getting so big," Forest said.

"Yes, he is. He is looking like you more every day," Anna said.

• • •

Sara sat near her window. She knew that it was near Christmas. But even Christmas would be no different than any other day to her. She was thankful for her dance slippers, coat, gloves, and jewelry box. She thought of the kind stranger that got her the slippers. Old Doc did his secret knock on the door. Sara was no longer hiding behind the veil she used to wear in front of him.

"Good day, my sweet Sara," Old Doc said.

"Good day to you too," Sara said with a warm smile.

Something in Sara was changing. Every time Doc came to see her he saw more and more glimpses of the old Sara shining through.

"Doc, do you think you could examine me first today?" Sara said.

Chapter 6

"I need to talk to you about something," Sara said. The look on Sara's face told Old Doc it was something of an extremely important nature.

"First, I will examine you; then we will eat; then we will talk," Old Doc said. "I have brought a special lunch today. Now let's look at that pretty face of yours." He actually got a giggle out of Sara. Sara looked him straight in the eye as he was examining her. "Your nails are starting to get some pink back in them. Those special treatments I have been giving you are working, Sara!" Old Doc's face was beaming. "Sara, your body is starting to heal," Doc said.

Sara then said surprisingly, "My heart and mind too."

Old Doc threw his arms around Sara. "Sara, my sweet Sara."

"So, what did you bring to eat?" Sara said jokingly.

"Well, Helena made you a special meal, Sara. All of your favorites: sliced turkey, gravy, sweet tea, cranberry muffins, and for dessert, apple pie."

All at once, memories of holidays passed came rushing through Sara's mind. Sara talked to Doc about how she and Helena used to string popcorn on the pine and evergreen trees for the animals. They thought they deserved a Christmas of their own too. She remembered singing Christmas songs around the Millers' piano and how Grandpa used to always read them *The Night before Christmas.*

"I miss everyone so much." Tears burst out of Sara's eyes. "I think…I think I'd like you to bring Helena on your next visit," Sara said.

"Oh Sara, my dear Sara, I'm sure she would love to see you!" Old Doc struggled through his own tears to find his voice. It was all Doc could have wished for this Christmas.

• • •

It was Christmas Eve, and everyone in town was working on Sara's gift. Ruth, Amy, and Helena were stringing popcorn. Pastor Peter, Little Ronnie, and Turner were looking for the perfect tree. Forest was working to carve out the last piece of wood. Anna and Mr. Fredrick were putting on the last touch of evergreen. Sister was wrapping gifts.

• • •

Sara was just waking up from a deep sleep when she thought she saw the flicker of candlelight coming toward her burnt-out fortress. She thought to herself, *Who would be coming to see me on Christmas Eve?* Old Doc and Helena would be attending Christmas service at this time. Suddenly, she heard the faint sound of singing. *It must be carolers from Gingerbread Landing coming through.* The beautiful singing was coming closer and closer to her. Soon it was right on top of her.

"Silent night, holy night. All is calm; all is bright." Even though it was almost midnight, there was a warm glow outside her window. The warm glow seemed to light up the sky like a fire.

Then suddenly she heard a voice speak that she knew very well. It was Old Doc. He said, "Sara, we love you, and we want you to know you are precious to us. Since you can't come to us for Christmas service, we brought Christmas service to you."

Then the pastor said, "Sara, after we leave here tonight, please come outside. There are some gifts waiting for you." Sara was speechless. Then Pastor began the service. "Praise be to God, maker of heaven and earth. May the Lord's peace be with you tonight, Sara." He then read the Christmas story.

Then Sara heard a voice she somewhat recognized. The voice said, "I'm Turner Thomas, Sara. I'm the one that gave you the dance slippers. I Hope you liked them."

Sara didn't know what to say to the man who gave her the greatest joy that she had in quite a long time, so she remained silent. Everyone could feel the electricity between him and her. It made the air thick with excitement.

The pastor's wife then started singing. Everyone joined in. Sara too started to sing. Sara peeked out the window. Only Doc and Turner noticed her. Everyone else was wrapped up with the night's festivities. Sara saw a beautiful sight: her friend's faces lit by candlelight. Everyone looked like angels. It was a sight Sara longed to see. The faces of her beloved friends. Sara couldn't even begin to imagine the other surprises that were in store for her that magical night. Sara noticed how bright the stars were shining that evening. A touch of God's hand over Summerville Heights. Sara could even picture the angels in heaven singing praises over the celebration.

After they finished singing "Away in a Manger," Pastor said these words: "Psalms 105: Give thanks to the Lord, call on his name; make known among the nations what he has done. Sing to him, sing praise to him; and tell of all his wonderful acts. Glory in his name; let the hearts of those who seek him rejoice."

Then Turner said this prayer. It was meant to speak directly to Sara's heart. "Psalms 18: I love you, O LORD, my strength. The LORD is my rock and my fortress; my God is my rock, in whom I take refuge I call to the LORD who is worthy of praise and I am saved from my enemies."

Pastor then asked everyone in joining Kim in singing Sara's favorite song, "O Little Town of Bethlehem and "O Holy Night."

Everyone listened to Sara singing with all of her heart. Every time it got to the line "O holy night, the stars were brightly shining," Sara sang even louder, as if thanking the Lord for this beautiful night.

"Merry Christmas, Sara," Old Doc said.

"Merry Christmas to all of you, all my brothers and sisters too." Everyone rejoiced at the sound of Sara's voice.

"We love you!" they all shouted. Each and every one of them told Sara how special she was. Sara was overwhelmed by the feeling of love. Sara almost felt complete again.

One by one, they called to Sara and said goodnight. The candlelight dimmed, and Sara was alone with her thoughts.

Sara rushed to put on her new gloves and coat. She didn't think this night could get any better, but it did. She remembered what Pastor told her: "When we leave, go outside." Sara ran to the door and opened it.

"Oh, Jesus, thank you. Thank you. You do still love me; you still do care." Sara was surrounded by a feeling of love and Hope. Even though Sara thought she was alone, she was not. Helena hid behind a patch of thick pine. She just had to see Sara's reaction to her gift. She had to share Sara's joy of this night.

Sara was so unbelievably surprised! There, at her front door, was a beautifully decorated ever green, all strung with popcorn and penny candy. Then underneath the tree were beautifully wrapped gifts. The three gifts were wrapped in silver, green, and red paper and tied up with shiny red bows. Also under the tree was a small, wooden, hand-carved manger. She started to cry. But then she saw the best gift of all. It was Morning Dew. He had an evergreen wreath around his neck and a pretty red ribbon on his saddle. She dropped to her knees right there in the snow. She breathed a prayer of thanks. She wanted to ride Morning Dew, but she also wanted to open the other gifts. She opened the gifts first. It was the dress, pocketbook, and hat Kim made, and the tablecloth and blanket. She didn't know if she could take much more excitement. Her hands were shaking, her heart was racing, and there was a bit of sweat rolling off her forehead. Helena, still secretly waiting in the trees, wanted to run to Sara but did not know if Sara was ready to see her without her veil on. She said a quick prayer and left Sara to be alone.

Sara climbed up on Morning Dew. She felt just like a child again. Sara gave a light touch to Morning Dew, and he took her down Happiness Trail. She remembered the story of her father telling her how him and Mama found this dirt road soon after they got married and named it Happiness Trail. The snow falling lightly again, Sara stuck out her tongue and tasted it. The cold wetness felt good. Sara took in the sights and smells of Happiness Trail. It was as though Morning Dew still remembered Sara's favorite oak tree. He stopped in front of it. Her daddy planted it when he found out her mother was pregnant with Sara. Every summer her daddy and her had a secret picnic under it. Her daddy used to say, "This is your tree, Sara." She then saw the field where she got her first kiss; the memory was a bittersweet one. Sara then saw the berry bush her and her mother used to pick from. Sara let her mind and spirit get lost in all the wonderful memories.

• • •

Little Ronnie was still wrapped up in the events of Christmas service last night. He was not even disappointed that he did not get a Christmas gift this year.

Kim set the table, pouring tea from a silver teapot for Grandpa and Turner. Ronnie and Mr. Frederick left early to go to the general store and post office.

Turner said, "I sure think that last night lifted Sara's spirit."

Grandpa said, "Turner, you came to town and you are changing lives."

Turner said in reply, "I'm not; God is." Turner was a very humble man. He always gave glory to God.

Ronnie and Mr. Frederick arrived at the general store full of snow. Their faces were bright red. "Come; let me pour you some hot cocoa," Anthony said.

"Thank you," Mr. Frederick said in a clear voice. Both Ronnie and Anthony were impressed on how well Mr. Frederick was learning the English language.

The three men could not stop talking about last night. The buzz was all around town.

Just then Helena walked in to get her mail. She greeted everyone warmly. She then shared how she waited after everyone left to see Sara.

"Did you talk with her?" Ronnie asked.

"No, but I did see her ride down Happiness Trail on Morning Dew," she said.

The men were so very happy.

Mr. Frederick wanted to ask Helena to dinner this evening but did not want to in front of the other men. He waited till Ronnie went to load the wagon, and Anthony went to the stock room. He then said to Helena, "Miss Helena, would you do me the honor of accompanying me to dinner this evening?"

Helena replied in a soft shy voice, "It would be my pleasure." She was batting her eyes at him. They had been sweet on each other for many years. Mr. Frederick said, "Shall I ask Miss Kim to set an extra place at the dinner table tonight?"

"No, I will make dinner for you, and we shall eat in the stable by candlelight," Helena replied.

Mr. Frederick was pleasantly surprised. "Shall we say 6 p.m. then?" Mr. Frederick asked.

"That will be fine," Helena replied.

Just then Ronnie came in and said, "Wagon is loaded." Anthony came back from the storeroom, and the men said goodbye. Mr. Frederick gave a wink to Helena. Ronnie and Anthony held back a chuckle. They knew that Mr. Frederick and Helena were in love. The town had been waiting for Mr. Frederick to court Helena for many years too.

· · ·

"Anna, baby John is getting so big," Forest said to his wife.

"Yes, he is. I can't believe he is already almost six weeks old," Anna said, looking down lovingly at her little boy. "Papa Bear, I wonder what he will be like when he's grown up."

"Well, Mama Bear, with a mama like you, he is going to be a fine young man," Forest said, teasing his wife.

"Oh, Papa Bear, you little devil you," Anna said; then she threw her arms around him and kissed him. Just then John cried a hungry cry.

"Well I guess it's time for feeding," Forest said with a smile.

· · ·

Ruth sat in her ice cream parlor wondering what she could do to help Sara. "I know, dear Lord, that you hear my prayers. Please guide me in my step to help Sara," she prayed. She was lost in thought, so she did not notice Old Doc Benson standing right in front of her. "Oh, I'm sorry. I did not see you there," Ruth said.

"It's okay; sometimes I get lost in my own thoughts too," he replied.

"So what can I do for you?" Ruth asked.

"Well, I've come to get some sweet treats for Sara. I'm going to see her this afternoon. I'm also going to bring Helena. Sara requested to see her," he said.

"That is really wonderful," Ruth said with a glow.

"Yes, I think Helena might just be the one person that can convince Sara to go see the doctor in Paradise Gates."

"I really Hope so. I prayed so hard for that," Ruth said.

"Me too," Doc said.

"Sara would have her life changed if she would go," Ruth said.

The little bell on the door to the ice cream parlor rang. Ruth and Old Doc looked up to see who it was. It was Helena. She greeted them with a warm smile.

"When I saw Healer outside, I figured you were here. I need to talk to you about Sara," Helena said to Old Doc.

"It is funny you should mention Sara. I need to talk to you too about her. But ladies first," Old Doc replied.

"Well, yesterday after everyone left, I stayed behind. I watched Sara behind a patch of trees; she looked so happy. I saw her riding Morning Dew."

"You did, really?" Ruth said.

"That's wonderful," Old Doc said. He then went on to say, "Helena, the last time I saw Sara, she asked to see you. I am going to see Sara today. Would you like to come with me?"

"Oh yes, Doc. How I longed to run to Sara yesterday and put my arms around her," Helena cried.

"Helena, please understand that Sara is still in a very fragile, vulnerable state of mind, so I think it's best if we keep our visit short," he told her.

"Yes, Doc, I promise you I will," Helena said.

"Well, I think we best be going," Doc said to Helena. They said goodbye to Ruth.

• • •

Pastor Peter was writing his sermon for Sunday. Still excited about the events of yesterday, he had a hard time concentrating on writing it.

"Dear, would you like a spot of tea?" Amy asked her husband.

"Yes, I think that would warm me up," Pastor replied.

Amy went into the kitchen that doubled as a guest room. She warmed the tea. Her mind too was on Sara. She rejoiced in the memory of yesterday.

"Dear, would you like some vanilla wafers to go with that?" she called from the kitchen.

"Just the tea will be fine," the pastor called back.

Amy Carrie kept her husband company as he sipped his tea. Pastor and Amy discussed what else they might do to help Sara.

"It is going to be a cold, long winter," Pastor said. "Sara will not be able to keep warm in that house," he added.

"Yes dear, but she will never leave it," Amy said. "If only there was something we could do to make the house warmer."

"Amy, please join me in saying a prayer that we will find a way to solve this problem."

Amy and Pastor joined hands and said these words, "Corinthians 2:13; praise be to God and father of our Lord, Jesus, the father of compassion and the God of all comfort who comforts us in our troubles, so we can comfort those in any trouble with the comfort we ourselves have received from God."

• • •

Sister Victoria sat in her rocking chair darning some socks. She had stew cooking over the fire for supper. Even though she was in pain with her hip, she still thought of Sara's pain. She would eat less tonight so she could save some stew for Sara. She rocked back and forth after she was finished darning her socks. She poured herself some stew.

. . .

Mr. Frederick and Ronnie had arrived home at the Miller farm. Mr. Frederick, excited about his date with Helena tonight, told Turner about it as soon as he saw him.

"Thank you, Turner," he said in his non-broken English.

Turner put his arms around him and said, "Just remember, at your wedding, I want to be your witness."

"Turner, aren't you getting ahead of yourself? This is just our first date," Mr. Frederick replied.

"There will be a wedding; just wait and see," Turner said, smiling.

Mr. Frederick smiled back.

Little Ronnie and Ronnie were unloading the wagon when Grandpa came out to help. "Just in time. I was going to go out looking for you. My bones are telling me a storm is headed our way," Grandpa said.

"Really? There is not a cloud in the sky," Little Ronnie said.

"Just wait and see; my bones have never failed me before," Grandpa said.

Kim was inside fixing ham steak, carrots, and turnips for supper. The warmth in her kitchen made her forget how cold it was outside. When she opened the door, a cold wind slapped her face. "You boys, dinner is almost ready," she said.

Mr. Frederick told her he would not be eating with them tonight. The men got washed up and ready for dinner.

They joined Kim at the dinner table. They said grace and began to eat.

Mr. Frederick paced around the stable nervously. It was nearly seven, and Helena had not yet arrived. Had she changed her mind? Had she realized he was just a poor immigrant from Poland who could not give her the life she deserved?

• • •

"Sara, I brought a visitor to see you today, so please prepare yourself!" Doc yelled through the window. Sara pulled the black veil over her face. She knew Helena was with Doc. She was not yet ready to let Helena see her face.

Helena held back tears as she entered the burned-out childhood home of her dearest friend.

"Helena, you're here." Sara ran to her friend, kissed, and embraced her. Sara looked into Helena eyes; she could always read Helena's heart by her eyes. Suddenly she stunned Helena and Old Doc by removing her veil. Before Helena had time to react, Sara said, "Helena, I know no matter what I look like I know you can and always have been able to see the real me."

The woman held on tightly to each other and wept. Helena then talked to her old friend. They lost hours talking about old times, childhood dreams, and things happening around town. The two women even lost awareness that Doc was in the room. Doc sat silently as the women talked.

Then he said, "Helena, I think Sara needs rest now. I think we should leave. Don't you have a date tonight that you were telling Sara and I about?"

"Oh my goodness! In all the excitement, I forget about

Mr. Frederick, and I didn't even make dinner," Helena said with a worried look.

"Don't fret, Helena; we had left over turkey and a fruit pie. You can bring them," Sara said.

"But Sara—" Helena said.

"I insist," Sara said.

"Oh, Sara, my dearest friend, may I come to visit you again soon?"

Then Sara said, "I wouldn't have it any other way." They all said goodbye.

Old Doc Benson took Helena to the Miller farm and then left. It was nearly 8 p.m. Poor Mr. Frederick was still in the stable waiting for his ladylove to arrive. Helena ran to the stable with excited breath.

"Oh, Helena, you are here. I have been worried sick," Mr. Frederick said.

"I'm so sorry, but once I tell you where I've been, you will understand," Helena said.

Mr. Frederick could not keep his eyes off Helena. She was a vision to him. She was wearing a purple dress that came down four inches below her knees, a shiny pair of Mary Jane shoes; her dress had pink trim along the collar and waist. When Sara found out she was going to see Mr. Frederick tonight, she insisted Helena wear her pearl necklace.

Mr. Frederick looked charming in his brown suit. He had picked winter's wild flowers to give to Helena; he wrapped the flowers in a pink satin ribbon. When he gave it to her, she blushed.

"You look beautiful, Helena," Mr. Frederick said.

"You look handsome," Helena said.

"So tell me, where have you been all this time?" Mr. Frederick asked.

Teasingly, Helena replied, "I went to see my boyfriend." Mr. Frederick looked concerned. "No, silly, I went to see Sara."

Under the moonlight, Helena told Fred all about her visit with Sara. Mr. Frederick listened with great interest. Helena saw that night the compassionate, gentle, caring man he was. After Helena told Mr. Frederick all about Sara, Mr. Frederick looked deep into Helena's eyes.

He said, "I've loved you from the moment I saw you, Helena." Mr. Frederick took her hand in his and said, "Helena Viola Smith, will you marry me?"

Helena said, "Yes, but not until our dear friend Sara can be my witness."

Mr. Frederick, being the loving man he was, said, "We are already joined by heaven's bond. I shall wait for you." Then he pulled Helena close and kissed her.

Helena's head spun from the undeniable magic of their shared first kiss. They looked up, and the big bright moon shared their Hopes and dreams for the future with them.

• • •

Anna, Amy, Kim, Ruth, and Helena met at church early on Sunday to discuss how to convince Sara to go see Doc William Olson, the doctor from Paradise Gates.

"Helena maybe on your next visit you can talk to her about it," Amy said.

"I will, but I don't know if it will do any good," Helena replied.

Pastor walked into the church and saw the women

talking. He greeted each one by name. "Service will be starting soon, so, ladies, you may want to take your seats."

The women all took their seats. Sister Victoria soon arrived at the church. She greeted each one of them with a warm hug. She then explained she had dropped off stew and corn bread at Sara's doorstep.

"Oh, Sister, in this cold, I wish you would have told me," Ruth said.

"Do you have enough to eat?" Ann asked.

"Man can't live on bread alone, but on every word that comes from the mouth of God," Sister replied.

"Amen," the assembly said.

Just then, Turner, Grandpa Miller, and Little Ronnie arrived at the church.

"Good morning," Turner said.

"Good day," they all responded. Little Ronnie took a seat next to his mother.

Turner spoke a few moments to Pastor before taking his seat. Old Doc Benson soon came, followed by Forest and Anthony and then Mr. Frederick. Mr. Frederick had a huge smile on his face. Helena had not revealed that last night they got engaged. Mr. Frederick slid into the pew next to Helena.

Pastor then began the service. Pastor Peter said, "God is good."

All in the church responded, "All the time."

Then Pastor said, "Please open your Bibles to Romans 8:18." Then he read these words from it: "I consider that our present suffering are not worth comparing with the glory that will be revealed in us."

All knew he was talking about Sara's suffering and how Christ died on the cross so no man would have to suffer again. The church responded, "Amen." After Pastor Peter gave his sermon, there was once again a renewed spirit in the church to help Sara.

"*Amazing grace, how sweet the sound,*" Amy and Anna started to sing. Soon the whole church joined in.

Mr. Frederick could not keep his eyes off his beautiful Helena. While they were singing "Amazing Grace," he thought to himself how truly blessed he was. After they finished singing, Mr. Frederick, in his overwhelming happiness and awesome thanksgiving to God, sang these words: "Then sings my soul, my Savior Lord, to thee; how great thou art."

Everyone saw the happiness in Mr. Frederick's eyes. They began to sing with him. Their soulful voices filled the church and the air outside with sweet praises to heaven. Pastor Peter then said, "Shout with joy to God, all the earth! Sing the glory of his name; make his praise glorious! Psalms 66."

Pastor ended the service with a blessing.

Mr. Frederick and Helena could no longer wait to make their happy announcement. Before everyone left to go over to the fellowship hall, Mr. Frederick and Helena stood side by side, holding hands, and told about their glorious engagement.

"The Lord hears our prayers," Pastor said.

Ruth said, "Congratulations!"

Anna grabbed Helena and kissed her. Everyone was caught up in the feeling of love and warmth for the happy couple. One by one, they sent blessings on their engagement.

"When is the big day?" Grandpa asked Mr. Frederick.

"We don't know yet. Helena and I agreed not to get married until Sara can be our witness."

Ronnie then said, "It just would not be the same without Sara. I'm glad you're waiting."

Ruth said to them, with a wide-toothed smile, "Bless you for your concern about Sara."

Mr. Frederick then revealed another surprise to everyone. He told them how Turner taught him to read and write and speak proper English.

Turner was very modest and said, "God was the teacher. I was only the messenger of God's helping hands."

All stood amazed by Turner's modesty. Everyone entered the fellowship hall for another fabulous feast. Pastor blessed the food. As they were eating, Turner came up with another idea to help Sara.

"If Sara won't go to Paradise Gates to see Dr. Olson, can't we bring him here?" Turner asked.

"Yes, Turner, but if Sara goes through with the surgery, she must go to Paradise Gates because they have all the medical equipment there to help her. I do not have that in my small office," Doc said.

Then Anna said, "Won't that surgery be more than what we can afford?"

Old Doc responded, "Maybe quite so, but maybe the doctors there will do the surgery out of the kindness of their hearts."

• • •

Sara danced around her house in the slippers Turner gave her. She could not stop thinking about the events of the past two months. As she prayed, these thoughts and words kept coming and speaking to her heart: "by his stripes we are healed." She thought more and more about going to Paradise Gates to speak with the doctors there. *Next time Helena comes I will talk to her about it,* she said to herself.

• • •

"Grandpa, are you feeling okay? You have been coughing quite a bit," Turner said in a concerned voice.

"Just the cold winter air," Grandpa responded.

Ronnie looked at his father with a heavy brow. "Still, I will take you into town to see the doctor tomorrow. "

"Son, you worry too much," Grandpa said.

Kim poured hot tea into a cup for Grandpa.

Ronnie said "Little Ron, you take Grandpa to his room; help him to bed. I insist that he doesn't work on the farm today."

"Son—" Before Grandpa could finish, Little Ronnie was taking Grandpa to his room.

"I'm worried about him; he works too hard," Kim said.

"I am too," Ronnie said.

"Kim and I shall fix him a mustard rub until he can get to see Old Doc," Turner said.

Mr. Frederick added, "I shall get my blanket from my room so Grandpa can keep extra warm tonight. Turner and I will get extra wood for the fire too; it looks like a nasty storm is coming."

"Dad you stay here. Mr. Frederick, Turner, and I shall attend to the farm and you attend to Grandpa, okay?" Little Ronnie suggested.

"Yes, son, that sounds like a good idea," Ronnie said. Ronnie was very grateful to have been blessed with such a responsible son.

Chapter 7

Sister Victoria sat as close to her potbelly stove as she could get.

"Old man winter is sure angry today," she said to herself out loud.

She was sipping tea and eating warmed-up, day-old corn bread. After she finished her tea and ate her corn bread, she decided to read a book Old Doc gave her from his medical library about childbirth. Sister Victoria was always fascinated about how big-city doctors were always coming up with new concepts to ease a woman's labor pains and make childbearing easier.

"Old ways are the best, except when it comes to Sara's medical problems," she said in thin air.

• • •

Ruth was pacing back and forth in her little apartment behind her ice cream parlor. *With days like these, no one needs ice cream. Maybe it's time to consider that offer. No, it would be impossible for me to even consider it.* Thoughts filled her mind. The wind howled outside her window.

• • •

"Listen to that wind, Papa Bear," Anna said to her husband. Mountain people were used to storms but never heard wind like that before. Anna wrapped her coat around John Michael to keep him extra warm.

"I sure Hope it does not snow while I'm at work tomorrow. I will never get home," Forest said.

"Yes, I know, Papa Bear," Anna said.

• • •

Anthony was gathering up supplies to bring to Sara's doorstep to get her through this winter's night. He made her a basket and filled it with soup, muffins, cream of wheat, tea, and a large piece of firewood. Then he added a lantern too.

"If we get a snow storm, these supplies will keep her warm for a few days," he said, talking to God. Anthony was putting the saddle on little friend when from behind him he heard Old Doc's voice.

"Hello, Anthony," Old Doc said.

Anthony turned around. "Hello, Doc," Anthony replied.

"Where are you headed?" Old Doc asked.

Anthony answered, "To Sara's doorstep with these supplies."

"I was on my way there too. With the storm coming, I don't want Sara to be alone. Since I'm headed that way, I'll take the supplies. You can check on Ruth and Sister Victoria," Doc replied.

"Sounds like a mighty fine idea to me," Anthony agreed.

"Okay; if anyone is looking for me, tell them I'm at Sara's then," Old Doc said.

"Okay. I want you to be careful, Doc," Anthony replied.

"I will; you be careful too," Doc said. Then he was gone.

• • •

Helena did not want to spend this cold winter's night alone. She knew Sister's door was always open, so she decided to go there. Just as soon as she reached Sister's door, the cold turned blizzard-like and the snow began falling heavily.

• • •

Amy and Pastor would hold a prayer vigil tonight for all their friends to be safe and keep warm. If they were going to get caught up in a heavy snowstorm, the church was warm and they would be safe there. Pastor knew the others would come there too if the storm got bad. The old church endured many heavy snows, angry windstorms, and wicked, wild weather. It had survived two hundred fifty years and would survive this storm too.

• • •

Little Ronnie held wet cloths to Grandpa's head. "It's not working, Mom. It's not working; he is still burning up," he said in a panicked voice.

Mr. Frederick went to get Old Doc.

"Little Ronnie, everything will be all right," Kim said in a calm, reassuring voice. Turner silently prayed over the man he had come to adore as his own grandfather. Ronnie tried to be a tower of courage for his family even though he was worried sick.

• • •

Forest, Anna, and baby John Michael went to the church for shelter. They joined Pastor and Amy in prayer that this storm would pass quickly. The wind wrapped against the church stain-glass windows like an angry spirit.

Ruth and Anthony rode double back on little friend to the church. They no longer felt safe in Ruth's tiny two-room apartment. Ruth, never easily shaken, was glad when they arrived in the shelter of their Father's home. Anthony told everyone that Old Doc had gone to stay with Sara. They were all relieved Sara would not be alone this night. The friend's prayed for his safe arrival to Sara's house.

Helena and Sister decided it was much too dangerous to travel to the church, so they prayed together at Sister's house.

• • •

Old Doc arrived at Sara's before the heavy snowfall hit Summerville Heights. He found Sara shivering under her blanket. With no fire and just pieces of spare wood as a roof and shelter, she would have frozen to death if Doc had not come. Old Doc quickly built a fire and fed her soup and tea. "I'm glad you are here, Doc," she said. "I always feel safe when you are here," she added.

"I'm glad I'm here too, Sara," Old Doc said. Just then, a burst of bitter cold air came through and blew the fire out Old Doc had built. So he quickly built another one.

• • •

Mr. Frederick, covered with snow and ice, burst open the doors of the church. He said with excited, winded breath, "Has anyone seen Doc?"

Anthony answered, "He is at Sara's."

"I need to find him. Grandpa is gravely ill," he said with a sad voice.

"Oh, my God!" Pastor cried.

They quickly decided the pastor would stay with Sara even if she did not want him to. Forest would stay at the church with the women. Anthony would go get Old Doc. Mr. Frederick would go check on his ladylove and Sister Victoria.

Ruth said, "Sara will never let the pastor stay with her; I'll go."

"No, Ruth, you must stay here," Anna said.

Ruth had made her mind up, and no one could stop her.

"There is no time to argue now. I must get Old Doc to Grandpa," Mr. Frederick said.

"Go, before it's too late," Ruth added.

Anthony said, "I will take Ruth with me, and then I will ride to the Millers with Old Doc with me."

Ruth had also made her up mind to tell Sara who she was, and tonight would be the night.

Pastor blessed them all, and they were on their way. The others continued to pray at the church.

• • •

Anthony and Ruth arrived at Sara's. Anthony yelled at Old Doc to come outside. So he quickly did.

"What are you both doing here? Are you crazy? You will freeze to death," Doc said.

Anthony, breathless, rapidly explained the situation to Doc. "But Sara will never let Ruth stay here."

To Anthony's, Ruth's, and Old Doc's surprise and amazement, Sara called through the open window.

"Yes, she can stay here. Now quickly go and save Grandpa."

Old Doc quickly yelled, "I will come back tomorrow!"

"Go, go! Hurry now, and save Grandpa!" Sara called back with urgency in her voice.

• • •

Turner stood over Grandpa's bed reading Scriptures to him.

"Come to me all of you who are weary and burdened. And I will give you rest. Take my yoke upon you and learn from me. For I am humble and gentle in heart and you will rest in me. Matthew 11: 28," he read.

"Turner, you know God's ways. What is heaven like?" Grandpa asked in a weak voice.

Kim had to walk away when Grandpa asked Turner that. She ran to the other room sobbing. Little Ronnie, trying to be strong like his dad, also had to run away.

Turner bent down and whispered something in Grandpa's ear. It brought a peaceful smile to Grandpa's face. "I knew. I have always known," Grandpa said, looking up at Turner.

Ronnie wondered what Turner said to bring his father so much comfort but decided not to ask. Grandpa then said, "Turner I want to talk to my boy alone."

"Of course, Grandpa, of course," Turner said.

• • •

Mr. Frederick finally arrived at Sister Victoria's house on Freedom after what seemed like an eternity. He slipped on ice walking to the front door. Sister heard a thump outside her window and thought a tree branch had broken. When Helena realized it was Mr. Frederick, she ran to the front door.

With heaviness in her heart, she asked, "What's happened? Is it Sara?" Her tears demanded answers.

"No, Sara is fine," he said. Sister Victoria sat him by the blazing fire. He began to tell them about Grandpa.

Helena let out a scream. "No! God can't take Grandpa away from us now." She cried.

Sister then quoted a Bible verse in Hopes of comforting Helena. Mr. Frederick held her tightly. She calmed down after a while. The three joined hands and began to pray.

• • •

Ruth sat quietly in front of Sara wearing her black veil. Ruth then began to speak. Before she could get out a sentence, Sara shook her soul with such force.

Sara said, "I know who you are."

"Well, of course you know who I am, Sara. I'm Ruth Brown, and everyone in town knows that."

"No." Sara's voice, unshaken, without anger or aggravation, went on to say, "I know who you really are. You are Larry's aunt."

"You…you do. I…I…didn't…" Ruth said, stumbling on her words.

"I have forgiven you a long time ago, but I have many questions about you." Sara said, looking Ruth straight in the eyes.

• • •

Old Doc and Anthony finally arrived at the Miller farm. Happiness Trail, now covered with snow and ice, was hard for even Healer to walk through. Anthony left Little Friend at Sara's in case the women needed him. Anthony quickly took Healer in to the stable, wiped him down, and got him warm.

When Old Doc Benson walked into the front door of the Miller home, he could see by Kim's tears Grandpa's situation was grim, very grim.

"Where is he?" Old Doc asked. Kim could not speak. All she could do was point to the back bedroom. Turner sat beside Kim and Little Ronnie, quietly comforting them. Old Doc found Ronnie, his hands in his lap, trying to be brave.

"Doc, I cannot lose him," he whispered.

"Ronnie go take a break; go get some coffee. I'll attend to Grandpa," Doc directed. Ronnie, refusing to leave Grandpa's bedside, would not move an inch. Kim then entered the room.

"Ronnie, come; do as Doc says," she said in a soft, supportive voice. Ronnie then got up and walked into the other room.

Grandpa's face was pale gray. His eyes looked like those of a wounded child. His labored breathing chilled Doc to the bone. Grandpa looked up helplessly at Doc. In a faint whisper, he said, "Doc, I know God is calling me home."

"Not tonight, not tonight," Doc said. He listened to Grandpa's shallow breathing and his rapid heartbeat. He knew Grandpa may not make the night.

• • •

"Sara, I'll try my best to give you the answers you seek. I will answer honestly, but I have never been able to interrupt Larry's heart," Ruth said.

"I never expected you to read Larry's heart. I was his wife, and I couldn't even do that," Sara said. "My first question is, when Larry was sick, why didn't you ever tell me you were his aunt?" Sara questioned.

"I didn't know how to, and I thought you would hold me responsible for Larry's actions." Ruth then explained how she came to know their marriage and about Larry's childhood.

"I never knew Larry's mother abandoned him," Sara said with compassion in her voice. "Why didn't you come see me after the fire, Ruth?" Sara asked

Ruth, now weeping, took Sara's hand. Sara did not pull her hand away. "Sara, you have lived in this prison after the fire, and I have lived in my own prison in my mind," Ruth sadly said.

Sara then began to weep. "Ruth, do you think Larry is sorry for causing us so much pain? Do you think he will ever turn himself in? Ruth, I have forgiven you, but I still cannot forgive Larry. Will you help me find forgiveness?" Sara wept harder.

Ruth, visibly shaken, said, "Sara, there is more I need to tell you." She then took out the folded note from Larry that she carried in her pocket. She then took a deep breath and read it to Sara.

"Ruth, is it real? Is it really a note from Larry?" Sara asked.

"Yes, my child yes," Ruth said.

"I must go and see for myself if he is truly sorry for doing this," Sara said, taking off her veil.

"Oh my child, oh my child, my poor precious child," Ruth said, never turning away from Sara's peeled skin and blackened face. "Larry is dead." Sara began to weep. Ruth put her arms around Sara.

• • •

"The snow finally stopped," Pastor said.

"Yes, but I'm sure it must be at least a foot out there," Anna said.

"Yes, but at least we are safe, and I'm sure the others are too," Forest said. Baby John began to cry. They began to laugh and forgot their worries for a moment.

• • •

Grandpa called everyone in one by one and started saying his goodbyes.

"We are not giving up and neither are you, okay dad!" Ronnie said.

Grandpa shook his head. "Ronnie, I'm ready to go, and I have lived a good life."

"No dad, we need you here," Kim cried.

Anthony said to Turner, "I need to get the others; he wants to say goodbye."

Turner said, "I will go too."

"No, you stay here; they need you. They will fall apart without you," Anthony said.

"But are you going to be okay?" Turner asked, concerned.

"Yes, God will be with me. God will be my strength," Anthony said.

"Your strength and your shield," Turner said. Turner then returned to Grandpa's bedside. Old Doc was doing all he could for Grandpa.

Turner said these words to Grandpa, "Psalms 73:26: 'My flesh and heart may fail, but God is the strength of my heart and my portion forever.'" With that, everyone began to cry.

Grandpa then said, "Don't cry. I'm going to paradise."

Anthony first told Mr. Frederick, Helena, and Sister the news. They rushed to Grandpa's bedside. He then rushed to see Ruth and Sara.

Sara, remembering all the kindness Grandpa had shown her, could not abandon in his time of need. She covered her face, hands, and legs, and her and Ruth rode double back on Little Friend to the family farm.

Anthony then got to the church and told everyone. They rushed to the farm.

Inside they saw an incredible scene: Sara covered with black material from head to toe to hide her burns standing over Grandpa's bedside, reading Scripture, fighting her own pain to ease Grandpa.

• • •

Officer Danny packed his bags to make his long journey to Summerville Heights. He must get this letter to Sara Wilson. He kissed his wife goodbye. He said to her, "I'll see you in a few weeks."

"God speed," his wife said. Officer Danny got on his black horse and started toward Summerville Heights.

· · ·

Sara sat at Grandpa's bedside; all eyes were on Sara. No one dared speak.

"Sara, come closer. I must talk to you," Grandpa said in his weak, faint voice. Grandpa looked around the room. He saw everyone staring at him and Sara.

"Leave me be with Sara," he said in a mere whisper.

Everyone quietly left the room. Sara and Grandpa spoke for hours. No one stepped foot inside the room. Sara then kissed Grandpa on the forehead and said good-bye. She knew this would be the last time she ever saw him. After stepping out of the room, ignoring everyone else there, she directly walked over to Doc.

"I need to go home and think. I need no visitors for a few days. Will you please ask everyone to respect that?" she said, whispering in his ear.

"Yes, of course, Sara," Doc said, swallowing a huge lump in his throat. The snow was starting to melt a little. Doc knew Sara would be okay going home. Sara left without looking back at anyone, leaving them speechless. Old Doc told everyone what Sara said.

One by one, Grandpa called them in. They all talked until there were no unspoken words between them. The women had tears in their eyes, and the men comforted the women. Pastor was the last one in to see Grandpa. He read Scripture, blessed Grandpa, and told him it was time to go. He then came out of Grandpa's room and announced Grandpa had gone to be with the Lord. Suddenly the house became full with tears, rage, and anger. Pastor tried to calm them down but couldn't. Pastor himself was in great pain.

Turner's voice got their attention. "Friends, we know Grandpa is in paradise; let us not weep or be angry." Then he read this passage to them: "John 14:1: 'Do not let your hearts be troubled. Trust in God; trust also in me. In my Father's house are many rooms; if it was not so, I would have told you. I am going there to prepare a place for you. I will come back and take you to be with me that you may also be where I am.'"

• • •

"Summerville Heights. I guess I'm here," Officer Danny said. *This town seems more deserted than even my town,* he thought to himself. He went down Happiness Trail, found Sara's house, and left a box at her doorstep. He then turned around and headed right back to Shady Woods.

• • •

Sara, exhausted from last night, slept all morning and afternoon. When she finally awoke, she hoped that last night had never happened. Then, as the sunlight shined on her face, she remembered it all: Ruth's face, the letter, and, worst of all, holding Grandpa Miller's hand for the last time. She stretched her arms and made something to eat. Over and over, Grandpa's last words to her replayed in her mind: *God will give you beauty for your ashes.* She couldn't get the words out of her head.

Although she could not remember much about the fire, she remembered Larry standing over her. "Why did he do it, God? Why did he leave me to die? Why did he hurt me so much when all I tried to do was be a good wife?" Although she wanted the answers, she would probably never get them.

Chapter 8

It was Sunday. The snow was all melted, the sun was shining brightly, but no one would ever feel the warmth of the sun today. Today everyone sat in black suits and dresses, mourning Grandpa.

Precious Blood United Methodist Church; The church was filled with tears. Pastor Peter walked, looking down to his pulpit. He began the service with a blessing. He then talked about Grandpa's life. He then asked family and friends to come to the pulpit to share a special memory or story about Grandpa. The weeping began to subside when they started remembering Grandpa's life, how kind he was, and how strong his faith was.

Pastor ended the service with a Scripture reading from Thessalonians. "Brothers, we do want you to be ignorant about those who have fallen asleep, or grieve like the rest of the men who have no Hope. We believe that Jesus died and rose again, and we also believe that God will bring with Jesus those who have fallen asleep with him."

Turner then said, "I would like to add something to the memory of Grandpa Miller's life. He was not only a kind and faithful servant of God, but an angel here on earth." His deep affection for the man he only knew for a short time reflected strongly in his words.

The friends and family of Grandpa Miller then laid him to rest on the farm he loved so much beside his wife.

• • •

"Dear Mrs. Brown, I regret to inform you that without the funds, I will not be able to grant your request. Although I have much sympathy and concern for this young woman, you must understand the cost of the medical needs does not allow me to grant your request. At a future date, if you are able to come up with the funds, I shall do everything in my power to help this dear young woman. God's blessings, Dr. William Olson."

Ruth knew now what she must do. She got out her finest sheet of writing paper and sat down and wrote a letter.

• • •

Sara walked out to check and see if there were any packages left on her doorstep. It was Sunday, and usually somebody would drop off a package for her then. As she looked down, she noticed a small package on her doorstep. She did not recognize the handwriting. She bent down to pick up the package and brought it inside.

"I wonder who it could be from. Well, I guess there's only one way to find out," she said to the thin air. She opened the package. Her face turned pure white when she saw what was inside: Larry's wedding band. It was a silver plain band. There was also a picture of him and Sara on their wedding day and two small handwritten letters. Sara could not read what the letters said. She would have to wait for Old Doc to read it to her. She then looked at her own wedding picture. She then said all the things to it that she could not say to Larry in person.

• • •

Ronnie sat touching his father's Bible, reading his father's favorite Scriptures. He rocked back and forth in his father's rocking chair. He could still smell his father's cologne in the room. He could still picture his father walking in with his overalls on after working a hard day on the farm.

"Ronnie, come eat. It's not going to do you a bit of good if you get sick on us too," Kim said lovingly.

"Yes, Papa, come eat," Little Ronnie said.

Ronnie, still walking around in a daze, found his way over to the table. He forced down some ham and collard greens.

"Turner and Mr. Frederick will be back soon. They have gone into town to bring eggs to the general store," Kim said.

"But that is grand." He caught himself, then broke down and cried. Kim put her arms around Ronnie, and said, "It's okay, dear. Grandpa is proud of how you are running the farm. It's your farm now." Ronnie then smiled.

• • •

Turner and Mr. Frederick ran into Old Doc on the way to town. Doc had told them he was on his way to see Sara.

"I can't believe baby is six months old already," Forest said to Anna.

"Yes, pretty soon he will be walking," Anna said.

"Da, Da."

"Did you hear that, Anna?" Forest excitedly asked.

"Da, Da." John Michael then reached out for his father. Forest and Anna picked up John and danced around the room. They had just heard John Michael's first words.

• • •

Old Doc arrived at Sara's house; he had some really good treats for Sara today.

When he went into Sara's house, she was still staring at her wedding picture.

"Sara, I thought all the wedding pictures were destroyed in the fire," Old Doc said.

"This package came this morning. When I opened it, it had the picture, Larry's wedding band, and two letters," Sara said. "Can you please read the letters"?

Old Doc said, "Of course, my dear. Do you have them?" Sara handed Old Doc the letters. The first one read: "Dear Mrs. Sara, I am the officer from Shady Woods jail. Your husband turned himself in nearly three years ago. He asked me, in the event of his death, to please get this to you. I am sorry for your loss. Please know Mr. Larry did try to change his ways and in his last days found peace with God. He was extremely regretful for what he did, and he always spoke of you as his one true love. God's blessings, Officer Danny.

The second letter was from Larry himself. With his heart beating out of his chest, Old Doc read Larry's word to Sara.

"My dearest Sara, I know I do not deserve your forgiveness for what I have done, but I need your forgiveness. Sara I want you to know I was sick, but deep down inside I always did love you. I tried to come back. I tried. I will always regret it. Sara, do not punish yourself for my actions. You deserve happiness—the kind of happiness I could never give you. I asked God's blessings on your life, and I pray you will remember what happened on that awful night. If you find the truth, you will forgive me. Love, Larry."

"What is he talking about, 'if you find the truth'? We all know he is a monster and what he did to you." Doc's voice was filled with righteous anger. "Sara, I think you need to put this away and never read it again," he went on to say.

"Doc, do you think Larry did change and was sorry for what he did?" Sara asked, Hopeful.

"Yes, I do believe he was sorry, but the only truth about that night is he tried to kill you. We are not to judge; there is one who is only honorable enough to do that, but please, Sara, do not retrace that awful night in your mind," Old Doc demanded. "You need to move on past that night," Doc continued.

"Okay, Doc, we will not retrace that night. Now what have you got in the bag?" she asked. Sara was trying to put the questions of that night out of her mind, but Larry's letters only made the questions rise higher.

"Well, I've, got a peach pie, turkey, sugar cookies, and sweet tea," Doc said.

"Good, let's eat," Sara replied.

They ate. And then Sara said, "Old Doc, I need to know what really happened that night. I cannot remember. The only thing I can remember was Larry standing over me and the smell of my burning flesh." Sara sighed.

"Sara, you must not go back to that awful night. It will only cause you more pain. Sara, please promise me," Old Doc said.

"Doc, I need to talk to you about something else. About the doctor in Paradise Gates," Sara said.

"Have you decided to come to Paradise Gates with me Sara?" Old Doc said, trying not to give away the excitement in his voice.

"Well, I'm not saying yes yet, but I would like to know more about what they would do to help me." Old Doc then told her.

• • •

Ruth rushed to the general store to get the letter she had handwritten out in the mail.

"Well good day, Ruth," Anthony said.

"Good day to you too. This is a very important letter; this must go out in the mail today. I'm sorry I cannot stay to chat. I have something very important to do." Ruth then said goodbye and hurried out the door.

Anthony noticed the letter was addressed to a Mr. Bobby Landers in Sunrise, California.

Turner and Mr. Frederick arrived at the general store with some eggs and some fresh vegetables. Mr. Frederick ordered a special scarf for Helena and it arrived that day.

"Hello, gentlemen, how are you today?" Anthony asked with a caring smile.

"Seems strange that Grandpa is not making the delivery with me today," Mr. Frederick admitted.

"I know; I know. How are Ronnie, Kim, and Little Ronnie holding up?" Anthony asked in an understanding voice.

"As well as can be expected," Mr. Frederick replied.

Turner then said, "Suffering makes us closer to God.

God never promised us days without rain, but he did promise us strength for the journey."

The men were always very impressed by Turner's poetic way of speaking. The men then talked about Sara. They were still in awe of how strong her love for Grandpa was that brought her out of her dark fortress. Anthony then mentioned about Ruth and the letter.

• • •

Mr. Frederick wrapped the special scarf of green and blue material in pretty pink wrapping paper. It was his engagement gift to Helena. He then walked outside and put the saddle on Liberty. Liberty galloped down Happiness Trail.

He was soon in front of Helena's house. "Hello, my sweet," Mr. Frederick said in a jovial voice.

"Hello, my Freddy," Helena said.

He then walked up the stairs of her sitting porch and gave Helena a light peck on the lips. She then invited him inside. Helena and Freddie stood in front of a roaring fire. Freddy gave Helena her gift.

"I love it Freddy. I will wear it to church on Sunday," Helena said joyfully.

"I'm so glad." Fred smiled.

"But I didn't get you an engagement gift," Helena said with a worried look.

"Yes, you did Helena; you gave me your heart, and that's the only gift I will ever need," Mr. Frederick said tenderly.

"Oh Freddy," Helena said, wrapping her hand around his.

Chapter 9

Bobby Landers sat in his office behind his big desk. His office overlooked the ocean. On a clear day, out of his office window you could see streaks of white sand for miles and miles. He sat with a small white envelope in his hand. He took a sip from his coffee mug before opening it. Inside the envelope was a handwritten letter from a Mrs. Ruth Brown.

The letter read, "Dear Mr. Landers, if your offer still stands, I am ready to sell my ice cream parlor to you. It means a lot to me, but the reason I'm willing to sell it means a lot more. You can contact me with your decision at the following address: 777 Chilly Rock Lane, Summerville Heights, Georgia. Thank you. Sincerely, Ruth Brown."

Bobby Landers, a clean-shaven tall man with brown hair and hazel green eyes, only wore the finest tailor made suits. He met Ruth one year ago when he was traveling through Summerville Heights for real estate business. He made an offer to buy Ruth's ice cream parlor because he knew he could make a large profit on it. Bobby had a good business head but did not have a heart for people. When he bought a piece of land, he never cared about its history or its people, only if he could make a profit.

"So she wants to sell now. Well good. She will be

the first, and then the others will sell; then I can build my hotel." He grinned like the heartless Grinch himself. He took out a sheet of paper to write Ruth back. Bobby did not know about the story of Sara or how much the townspeople loved each other. He did not know that Ruth was giving up something she loved for someone she loved more. Even if he did, he would not have cared.

• • •

Sister Victoria sat on her porch on an unusually warm winter's day. It was February 20, 1904. Tomorrow was Little Ronnie's birthday. She sat on her porch swing making a special birthday present. Even though Little Ronnie had said he did not want to celebrate his birthday this year out of respect for Grandpa, Sister could not let it pass without making a gift for him. From the day he was born, she had been making a gift for every passing birthday. And she sure would not stop now.

• • •

Helena decided it was a beautiful winter's day. She would walk over to Sara's. She had gathered up some herbs and soup Sara could have for dinner. On the way over to Sara's house, she ran into Turner. He was going to deliver bread, potatoes, and fried chicken to Sara.

"Good day, Mr. Turner," Helena said.

"I'm just on my way over to Sara's to bring a basket Miss Kim had made for her," Turner said.

"Oh, that's funny. I'm on my way over there too," Helena said.

"Is it okay if I walk with you? I'd like to talk to you

about Sara," Turner explained. Turner then told Helena how he ran into Old Doc the other day and about the package Sara had received from the law in Shady Woods.

"Oh my, that must have floored Sara," Helena said with a very concerned look in her eyes.

"Yes, it did. Now Sara is wondering what really happened the night of the fire," Turner said. "I will leave you here so I won't scare Sara, but when you see her today, handle her heart with extra caution," Turner went on to say.

"How are Kim, Ronnie, and Little Ronnie holding up?" Helena asked.

"They are doing better. They are over the mourning process. I think God has healed their hearts," Turner said.

Helena then said, "Please tell them I will be by this week and I send my love."

• • •

Sara sat in her rocking chair enjoying the breeze. She then noticed Helena walking up toward the house. She was very excited to talk to her about the events of recent days and share a big decision that would change her life.

"Helena, I am glad that you are here. Please come and sit in my chair," Sara said with excited breath.

Helena told her about the goodies she had brought.

"Thank you. Helena, you are my best friend, so I wanted to tell you first. I have decided to go see the doctor in Paradise Gates," Sara shared.

"Oh, Sara, I'm so happy!" Helena said with tears running down her face. Then Helena, who had been waiting to share the news about her engagement, spilled the beans. Sara then dressed her face with the most beautiful smile.

The two friends wept and then talked about other events in town.

"I plan to tell Old Doc about my decision when he comes tomorrow. We will make the journey in the spring," Sara told Helena. Then Sara put her dance slippers on and danced for Helena. Just like they did when they were kids, Sara and Helena danced together once more just like Helena dreamed about.

• • •

Ruth waited anxiously for a response from Bobby, but none came. She wondered if Anthony remembered to put the letter in the mail. So she walked over and asked him.

Anthony said, "Sure did, Ruth. That letter must be mighty important to you."

Ruth then confided to Anthony why the letter was so important. "But you can't sell your parlor. That real estate man will tear it down, and it's too important to our town's history," Anthony begged. Just then, Turner walked into the general store to pick up supplies for Little Ronnie's birthday party.

"What's all this fussing about?" he asked. Ruth then told Turner.

"There's no need to sell your parlor. Tonight, after the party, I will go to Paradise Gates and talk to Dr. Olson myself," Turner said.

"But he already said he could not help Sara unless we came up with $5,000. And where are we going to get that kind of money from if I don't sell my parlor?" Ruth said bitterly.

"Leave it in God's hands. I will talk to the doctor," Turner said confidently.

"Okay, I will give you two weeks, but if you can't convince him, I will have to go through with my plan," Ruth explained.

"God doesn't need two weeks; he is working on a miracle now," Turner believed whole-heartedly. Turner got the supplies he needed then left.

Ruth and Anthony discussed that they wished they could be as confident as Turner was.

"I guess Turner has a special connection to God and that's where we fall short," Ruth said.

• • •

Ronnie and Kim sat at their kitchen table wishing that Grandpa could be with them at tonight's party. Mr. Frederick reminded them that he was looking down from heaven, so he would be. His comments brought a smile to both of their faces. Little Ronnie was outside cleaning the stable when Turner came back. Out of the corner of Turner's eyes, he saw Little Ronnie crying.

"Turner, why did God have to take Grandpa away? I need him here." Little Ronnie sobbed.

Turner replied sweetly, "Because God needed his angel back in heaven." That one little tender gesture immediately made Ronnie light up.

• • •

Amy Carrie was busy making a cake for Ronnie's party when Pastor got back from the church. He went there every day just to be alone with God for a while. When Amy looked at her husband's face, it seemed to be touched by the Spirit. Pastor Peter then said, "When I was praying,

God put it upon my heart that a miracle would be happening soon."

Amy then said, "I believe it." They both dropped to their knees and started to pray.

• • •

Old Doc Benson decided to take Morning Dew up to see Sara. Before Old Doc could even open his mouth, Sara wrapped her arms around him and said, "I'm going to do it. I'm going to see Dr. Olson."

Old Doc had tears pouring out of his eyes. "We must celebrate. I have Morning Dew here; let's ride him double, Sara."

As they rode Morning Dew down Happiness Trail, the birds were chirping and the sun was shining. Sara shared the secret memories of Happiness Trail with Doc.

• • •

It was the night of Little Ronnie's birthday party. Sister Victoria was the first to arrive at the farm. She gave Little Ronnie the gift she made. It was a memory quilt. Every patch was a different special memory Little Ronnie and Grandpa had shared. One patch was made out of Grandpa's overalls. It was the most special gift Sister had ever made for Ronnie.

The next to arrive were Forest, John Michael, and Anna. John Michael was starting to walk. Everyone was amazed on how big he had gotten. The next to arrive was Anthony, then Ruth, Pastor, Amy Carrie, and Helena.

The last to arrive was Old Doc. When he arrived, he was wearing a smile from ear to ear. The party had begun.

Everyone was eating, drinking, and in a good mood. They could feel the spirit of Grandpa there.

After they ate, Doc told everyone he had big news. So everyone gathered in the parlor to hear it.

"Sara is going to go to Paradise Gates in the spring. She is going to see Dr. Olson," Doc said.

Everyone cheered, except for Ruth and Anthony. Ruth hated to be the bearer of bad news, but she told everyone about the letter from Dr. Olson and how she was willing to sell her parlor to help Sara. Everyone was touched by her sentiments.

"But none of that is going to be necessary," Turner said. He then told everyone how he was going to leave tonight to go to talk to Dr. Olson.

"Do you think you can change his mind?" Ronnie asked with a raised brow.

"I cannot, but God can change men's hearts," Turner said.

"I will go with you," Doc said.

Turner responded, "No, I will need to make this journey alone. It will be best."

Everyone prayed for Turner, and then Ruth said, "You take Candy Apple with you. She is fast, she knows mountain territory, and she will be a help to you."

"Thank you," he said.

Ronnie and Mr. Frederick then packed supplies and hooked Candy Apple, Freedom, and Liberty to the wagon. Turner then left.

• • •

The next day Old Doc told Sara all that had happened.

Sara sat shocked and stunned. "You mean a man that

has never met me is going on that journey for me?" she asked.

Doc replied, "Yes, yes he is."

Days went by with no word from Turner. Ruth got a response from Bobby Landers that he was willing to meet her on spring's first morn to purchase her parlor. She prayed Turner could change Dr. Olson's mind.

• • •

Turner rode a narrow path. The snow had all melted, and spring hung in the air. There were new buds forming on apple trees and crape myrtle. The birds were returning, and there were signs of new life everywhere.

Turner entered the town called Paradise Gates. He could see why some called it paradise. It was a beautiful town. Big white houses lined the streets of the town; every house had a flower garden. Every house had a story to tell. There were cherry blossom trees, magnolia trees, and fruit trees everywhere you looked.

Turner could see the doctor's house in front of him just a few yards away. He prayed God would give him the words to touch the doctor's heart. He closed his eyes for a moment, and God gave him the words to use.

He pulled the team of horses and wagon in front of the doctor's house. It was a huge white house. It had a big iron fence around it and a huge iron gate. In front of the iron gate was a Sweet William tree. Just behind the iron gate was a long, twisted drive. Along the twisted drive were evergreen bushes.

Turner walked up the long, twisted drive to the spiral staircase leading to the front door. He rang the doorbell. He heard *ding dong* echo through the huge house. A man dressed in a black suit came to the door. Turner knew right away that it was Dr. Olson's butler.

"Hello," the lean man said. "May I ask who is calling for Dr. Olson?"

"My name is Turner Thomas. I come from Summerville Heights, and I was hoping Dr. Olson would have a moment to talk to me," Turner said with authority in his voice.

"The doctor is a very busy man, and he usually doesn't see patients without an appointment, but I'm sure he will make an exception for you," the man answered. "Come in, and I will see if he is available to talk with you now," the man continued. He then walked down a long hallway to get the doctor.

Turner found himself standing in a grand hallway. All around the hallway he saw fine art. A beautiful crystal chandelier hung above his head.

As he looked around, he heard a booming voice coming from behind him.

"Hello. Mr. Turner, I presume. I'm Dr. William Olson." The older gentleman was dressed in a fine suit. Turner guessed the suit was hand tailored in Italy. The man extended his hand out to Turner. Turner took his hand with a strong grip. "Mr. Pepper said you needed to speak to me," the doctor said.

"Yes, I do. I have come here from Summerville Heights, Georgia," Turner said.

"You came quite a long way just to see a doctor," Doc Olson replied.

"I have come to talk to you about a dear friend of mine. Her name is Sara Wilson," Turner went on to say.

"Oh yes, of course, the young lady that was burnt in that horrible fire," the doctor said.

"Yes, I know Ruth Brown has written to you about her," Turner said with a look of wisdom.

"Yes, she did. I already explained to her that the medical cost would be very high," Dr. Olson said. Turner then told the doctor how Ruth was willing to sacrifice the one thing that meant so much to her.

Doc Olson was very moved to hear about the love in Summerville Heights, Georgia, for sweet Sara. He normally would not have agreed to take on Sara's medical problems for free, but there was something about Turner, something that stirred the doctor's soul with compassion. After hearing Sara's story, the doctor agreed to do whatever he could to help her. He then gave Turner a bit of warning.

"I'm not going to say she will ever look the same, but we will do what we can, and, Turner, the road of recovery will be a very long one for Sara."

Turner then said a prayer of thanksgiving for the doctor's help. He said aloud, "'Teacher,' said John, 'we saw a man driving out demons in your name and we told him to stop, because he was not one of us.' 'Do not stop him,' Jesus said. 'No one who does a miracle in my name can say in the next moment anything bad about me, for whoever is not against us is for us.' Mark 9:38." The doctor suddenly knew by helping Sara he was doing the will of God.

Dr. Olson allowed Turner to stay for the night at his home. In the morning, he fed Turner and gave him supplies to go back home. Turner thanked the doctor for his hostility and then went on his way.

• • •

It was almost two weeks since Turner had left to see Dr. Olson. There was no word from him if he had convinced the doctor to take on Sara's case.

Ruth had begun packing, for she knew she would have to sell her beloved parlor.

Helena had offered her a place to stay until she could figure out what to do.

Pastor Peter was praying hard that God would choose now to perform his miracle.

Anna and Forest could not wait until Turner got home. They had been waiting to tell him that John Michael had spoken his first words.

Ronnie and Mr. Frederick waited too. They missed their brother. They missed working on the farm, in the soil of nature with Turner. Mr. Frederick was holding Hope secretly, for he knew as soon as Sara could be Helena's witness Helena would become his wife.

Anthony missed Turner's little jokes. Sister missed his smile.

• • •

Sara wondered in her darkness if she would ever feel the sun on her face again.

• • •

It was Sunday; everyone met at church. They were met by a familiar face. It was Turner. Two weeks to the day he left. No one could be more excited to see him than Ruth and Old Doc. Everyone waited with baited breath to see what Turner had to say. They tried to read Turner's expression, but not a line on his face would give away his secret.

They waited eagerly; then Turner said, "Psalms 41: 'Blessed is he who has regard for the weak; and the Lord will protect him and preserve his life. The Lord will sustain him from his sick bed and restore him from his bed of illness.'"

"Amen, amen. Praise God, all things under heaven and earth," Pastor Peter said.

"God is merciful indeed," Ruth said.

"Give thanks to the Lord for what he has done," Little Ronnie proclaimed.

One by one they praised God, for they knew God performed a miracle. They knew Doc Olson would perform one for Sara too. Amy started to sing "Oh Happy Day," and everyone joined in. Sara heard the joyful sound coming over the hills from the little white church.

She dropped to her knees and started singing her own praises to God. She knew from this moment on her life would never be the same.

"Let's all go tell Sara the good news, "said Old Doc.

"Yes, let's," Turner said. They all got on their horses and raced to Sara's house. They were all amazed when they saw Sara outside by her parents' graves weeping. Sara's back was toward them all. When she heard everyone coming, she turned around. Her face was not covered by the veil of shame. Instead it was covered with tears of joy. She immediately ran to Turner and embraced him. Then she said to all of her family and friends, "I don't have to hide anymore because you can see past my burns and see my heart." Everyone began to weep.

Chapter 10

It was the first day of spring when Turner, Old Doc, Sister Victoria, and Sara arrived in Paradise Gates. The town was blooming with new flowers, lush green grass, and new life. It was a magical time for everyone.

Forest and Anna just found out they were expecting another baby. Little Ronnie just started courting a girl named Holly Amber. Her parents, Summer and Adam Tinner, just moved to Summerville Heights. Pastor Peter and Amy were building on a new addition to their church. Anthony Joseph and Ruth started dating. Helena and Mr. Frederick were planning their wedding. Kim and Ronnie were getting more fruit, vegetables, and egg orders from Anthony and surrounding towns, more than they would have ever dreamed of.

It was a time of peace and prosperity in Summerville Heights. Everyone prayers were with Sara and the others.

"Sara, I'm Dr. Olson. I'm going to do everything in my power to help you."

Sara was scared to death but tried not to show it.

"I know this is going to be a very painful question, but can you tell me what you can remember about the fire?" he asked.

Old Doc's and Sister's faces dropped. They were outraged the doctor even asked a question like that. Sara answered the question honestly.

Sister Victoria and Turner were looking for a place to stay while they were in town. They came across a boarding house. The owner, Mr. Miles, said of course they could stay there.

Sara, Old Doc, and Sister were explaining the procedure that would take place in two days, for it would bring Sara back. Sara was excited but scared.

"What if the procedure fails? What if it makes me look worse than I do now?" Sara tried to put those fears out of her head. If was easy to do with her friends there with her.

Doc Olson would do a series of skin grafts on Sara, first on her hands, legs, and chest, then on her face. He would be assisted by Old Doc, his Nurse Lilly, and the head of Paradise Gates hospital, Dr. Friendsmore.

The first night in Paradise Gates came and went. Turner, Sara, Sister, and Old Doc had spent the night in prayer. In the morning, Mr. Miles fixed them steak and eggs for breakfast.

When Dr. Friendsmore had seen Sister Victoria walking with a cane, he had told her to come to his office after breakfast in the morning. The four friends headed to Dr. Friendsmore's office. It was located on the first floor of the four-story hospital.

When they arrived at the hospital, they were both intimidated by its size and fascinated by the special procedures performed there. On the first floor was Dr. Friendsmore's office. On the second floor a whole wing dedicated to woman having difficult pregnancies. The third floor was for the burn victims, and the fourth floor was dedicated to people who had lost their limbs, and special surgeries.

Turner said, "Yes, Sara you are going to come out of here a new woman. "

When Old Doc turned the doorknob to walk into Dr. Friendsmore's office, they were met by a kind gray-haired man. A mirror image of Old Doc himself. "Do I have a twin?" Dr. Friendsmore asked, laughing.

Old Doc said, "Great minds think alike, and I guess they look alike too." It broke the ice, and everyone laughed. One by one, they all introduced themselves.

Dr. Friendsmore then told them why he got in the business of medicine. "Sister Victoria, you remind me of my dear late mother, Francis. She had a bad hip too. She suffered with it all her life. I promised her I would help others like her, so I spent all my youth, time, and money inventing new ways to help. I came up with a procedure that replaces the bad hip with a new hip, and after I'm done with Sara's needs, I would like to give you a hip replacement." He said kindly.

"You are doing enough for Sara already," Sister said. Resultantly, she agreed to the hip replacement.

"Now I want you to all go home and get plenty of rest. Tomorrow will be a long day for all of us, especially you, Sara," Dr. Friendsmore said.

• • •

Helena ran to the church where everyone was meeting daily for prayer. "I've gotten a letter from Old Doc today," she said, excited.

"Read it; read it," said Little Ronnie. They all listened intensely as Mr. Frederick read the letter. It read: "Dear friends, Sara is doing well. She is having the surgery in two days. Sister Victoria will also be having surgery to correct her hip. Our prayers and love are with you. Love, Old Doc."

Everyone was so overwhelmed with emotion. Some cried, some cheered, and some prayed.

Baby John seemed to sum up everyone's emotions when he said, "Da, Da," looking up to the heavens. Forest looked down at his son and said, "That's right; it's in Da, Da's hands now." John Michael almost seemed to look at Forest as if he knew what he was talking about.

Pastor Peter led everyone in prayer. "Father, we come to you to ask your blessing over Sara's surgery. We ask you give Sara strength for whatever she must face, a steady skilled hand for her doctors, peace in Sara's heart, and understanding and wisdom in things yet to come."

• • •

In Paradise Gates, Dr. Friendsmore, Nurse Lilly, Dr. Olson, and Dr. Benson had one final meeting about Sara's surgery.

Sara and Turner and Sister Victoria prayed together. Sara prayed, "Give care to my words, oh Lord. Consider my sighing, listen to my cry for help, my King and my God, for you I pray. In the morning, oh Lord, you hear my voice. In the morning, I lay my request before you and wait in expecting. Psalms 51."

Sara laid her head on Sister Victoria's shoulder.

"Do you think all will go well?" Sara asked.

"Sara, God knows what we can handle and what we can't. God would not have brought us this far just to disappoint us," Sister replied.

Turner added, "Sara, the Lord himself knows every hair on your head. He will not let anything happen to you." Turner then spoke more about his life to Sara and Sister Victoria. He then said, "I have gone through disappointments, heartaches, triumphs, and tragedies, but the Lord has pulled me through them all."

Night fell on Paradise Gates. Old Doc soon arrived back at the boarding house. No one was able to eat much for supper that night. The four friends retired to bed early. Old Doc gave Sara a sleeping pill to help her relax that evening.

• • •

The chirping of crickets awoke Helena. "My dear Sara, my love is with you today."

On the Miller farm, the men stopped at sunrise to pray for Sara.

Anthony sat awake in his general store all night in case any letter came his way about Sara.

Ruth sat up all night reading Scriptures.

Holly Amber and her parents, the newest members of the Summerville Heights community, planted roses in thanksgiving of Sara's special day.

All the men at Forest mill stopped work and had a moment of prayer with Forest for Sara. Anna, Amy, John Michael, and Pastor were all at church praying.

• • •

"Sara, it is time to go," Sister Victoria said in a gentle, uplifting, motherly voice.

"I don't know if I can go through with it," Sara said.

"Yes, you can, Sara. God will give you the strength," Sister encouraged.

Old Doc and Turner got the horses and wagon ready. Sister helped Sara dress and wash, for she was still dazed from the sleeping pill.

Turner and Old Doc helped the women into the wagon.

On the way to Paradise Gates hospital, Sara could not help but notice that God was giving her signs that everything would be all right. She saw a yellow rose garden; yellow roses were her mother's favorite flower. She saw a tree just like the one her dad planted for her. She smelled the sweet fragrance of honeysuckle and jasmine, just like she did when she took early morning rides on Morning Dew. Most of all, she noticed a rainbow that stretched against a crystal clear blue sky.

"Look, a rainbow," Sara said. They took a moment to look at it, said a quick prayer, and then they were on their way.

Chapter 11

"Hello, Sara. Nurse Lilly will take you back to help you get ready, but first we will give you a moment with your friends," Doc Olson said in a warm tone.

Sara looked at Turner with tears in her eyes. "You did not know me, but you made me feel loved. How can I ever repay you for all your kindness?" Sara said softly.

"Be happy and be blessed; that's all I want," Turner said.

She then wrapped her arms around Sister Victoria. "All my life you have been taking care of me when mom and dad died and then with …"

Sister Victoria said, Hush, child, hush. I love you."

She then looked lovingly at Old Doc. "You are my happiness," Sara said.

Hugging Sara, Old Doc then said, "You will find even more."

Nurse Lilly was dressed in a pure white uniform, her hair pulled back tight under a hat. She was a young woman in her thirties. She was of a heavyset build, but she had the prettiest face Sara had ever seen. "Are you ready, Sara?" Nurse Lilly asked with a sensitive warm smile.

"As ready as I will ever be." Sara giggled nervously. Sara then hugged and kissed everyone, including Turner, and

Nurse Lilly took her back. Nurse Lilly took Sara into a sterile white room. There was a hard wooden table with a paper gown laying on it. Around the room were large machines, medical equipment, oxygen, and blood pressure cup.

Sara began to cry. "I can't do this!" she cried. She then saw a small little cross hanging on the wall. She then suddenly felt she was not alone in her fight. As soon as she changed into a gown, the nurse then tucked her hair under a blue hair net. She then gave Sara booties to put on her feet.

When she was ready, the doctors came into the room. She saw the Hopeful faces on them, which gave her Hope. Before they started the surgery, they all whispered a prayer.

Old Doc then said, "Sara, we are going to put this mask on you. You will start to feel sleepy. When you wake up, you will be covered in bandages, but under those bandages will be a new and improved Sara." Sara managed a smile.

Turner and Sister joined their prayers for Sara back with everyone else in Summerville Heights. Turner paced around the big waiting room of the hospital. Sister went down to the maternity ward to keep her mind off Sara.

• • •

Holly Amber sat under a tall oak tree, reading Scriptures from the Bible. She was a pretty red-haired girl with hazel green eyes. She had never met Sara, but she felt a strong sisterhood with her already. Holly Amber's one ambition in life was to be a dancer too. Her parents moved here from Gingerbread Landing, her mother, a seamstress, her father, a blacksmith. Holly had made many friends here in the short time she has been residing in Summerville Heights.

Her beau, Little Ronnie, was attracted to her lively spirit the first time he ever met her.

Summer Tinner, Holly's mom, was going to meet Helena later this afternoon to talk about making her wedding dress. Adam Tinner, Holly's father, was busy setting up his new blacksmith shop in the town square.

• • •

"Mama, hungry." Little John Michael looked up at his mother.

"You are one hungry little boy," Anna said. Anna fed her son some oatmeal.

"Yummy," John said with oatmeal stuck everywhere to his face. Anna laughed.

"Your daddy will be home soon. Let's get you washed up."

• • •

"She is asleep now," Doc Olson said.

"We may start," Doc Friendsmore replied. With a steady hand, they started the painstaking procedure of restoring Sara's broken body.

"How is her blood pressure, Nurse Lilly?" Old Doc asked.

"Holding steady," she replied. They restored the skin on her chest. Then they worked their way down to her arms and legs.

"My God, this is amazing. She is starting to look like the old Sara," Doc said.

• • •

Turner said, "I got us some coffee, Sister."

"Thank you. How do you think she is doing?" Sister asked with a shake in her voice.

"I promise you, Sister, she is fine. God has sent his angels to protect her," Turner said confidently.

"Yes, I know," she replied.

Old Doc came out of the operating room to give Turner and sister an update.

"Doc, is the news good?" Turner asked.

"Good, good—it's beyond good. We have our Sara back. We are working on her face now," Doc said joyfully.

"Thank you, Jesus, thank you!" Sister praised.

Doc then said, "I must go back in." Turner and Sister embraced and started singing praises to God.

• • •

Helena met Summer in the square to talk about the wedding dress. Helena was accompanied by Amy and Kim.

"What kind of dress do you have in mind?" Summer asked.

"I have always dreamt of a long, flowing, white, lace gown, with bell sleeves, and in the waist band would be a satin pink ribbon; the lace would have fancy rhinestones and pearls," Helena said dreamily.

"Well, I certainly think we can make your wedding gown dream come true," Summer replied. She then pulled out beautiful lace material, a package of pearls, and a pink satin ribbon. Then Summer said, "The only thing I don't have are the rhinestones."

"That's okay, Summer. It's still my dream come true," Helena replied.

Kim and Amy both said, "You will look like a princess." The women then took a break from planning the wedding and had some tea and butter cookies.

• • •

"Ruth, Ruth, I have a letter for you. It's from the law in Shady Woods," Anthony said, running toward her ice cream parlor.

"Why would they be sending me a letter?" she worried.

"Open it, Ruth, and find out," Anthony said with curiosity in his voice.

Ruth read the letter aloud. "Dear Mrs. Ruth, I am officer Danny, the officer your nephew turned himself into three years ago. I am writing to tell you I know the truth about what happened the night of the fire. I will be leaving Shady Woods to come to Summerville Heights to tell you the truth in the coming days. Thank you. Officer Danny."

"What is the truth?" Ruth said. Anthony just shrugged his shoulder in disbelief.

"Everyone in town thought they knew the truth about the fire. I will call for a meeting at church tonight. I will get the word to everyone to meet at the church at seven p.m.," Anthony said. "Sure. I will take Little Friend and start now," Anthony added.

"Oh thank you, Anthony," Ruth said, hugging him.

• • •

Old Doc came out of the operating room, smiling from ear to ear. "The operation was a success. Sara is fine. She is sleeping now," Doc announced.

"Oh that is so wonderful!" Turner said with tears in his eyes.

"Thank you, Father, thank you," Sister said, dropping to her knees. The three friends grabbed hands and started praying prayers of thanksgiving.

Nurse Lilly called out in a panicked voice. "Doctor, we need you. Sara's blood pressure has completely dropped!" Old Doc ran back into the operating room.

"Oh God, we can't lose her now," Sister cried.

"We won't lose her. She is in God's hands," Turner said, reaching out to Sister. Sister collapsed inside Turner's embrace.

• • •

Anthony got the word out to everyone to meet at the church. Everyone gathered at the church at seven sharp.

"Ruth, can you please tell us what this is all about?" Forest asked.

"Yes, I will, but I must warn you, this will come as a shock to all of you," Ruth replied.

Ruth then filled everyone in about the letter from officer Danny.

"What could he have to tell us?" Summer said.

"I don't know, but it won't do us any bit of good to speculate," Pastor Peter said. "Let us pray that it will bring peace to our hearts." Pastor then led them in prayer.

• • •

Doc Olson frantically said, "We are losing her!"

"No, we are not. I will not allow it!" Doc yelled.

"She has lost a lot of blood. We need to give her a

blood transfusion. Nurse Lilly, a bag of AB Negative, stat!" Doc Friendsmore ordered.

"Yes, doctor," Nurse Lilly replied. The doctors worked through the night to save Sara's life.

• • •

Officer Danny arrived in Summerville Heights with the truth its residents needed to know. Where would he begin though?

• • •

Mr. Frederick was out milking the cows. Ronnie was cleaning the stables, and Little Ronnie was collecting eggs when they heard Kim scream. They went running toward the house. "What is it, Mama?" Little Ronnie asked, concerned. Kim, white as a ghost, said with winded breath, "I saw Grandpa, and he was with, oh God, he was with Larry."

"Mama, all this talk around town has got you thinking you are seeing ghosts." Ronnie sat his pale wife down. Mr. Frederick poured her a glass of cool water.

"Honey, you only thought you saw them," Ronnie said.

"No, I did see them," Kim said in an argumentative voice.

"If you say you saw them, then we believe that you did see them," Mr. Frederick said, not wanting to upset Kim further.

• • •

Sister and Turner waited all night, without sleeping, for any word of Sara's condition. It was late morning when

Old Doc came out of the operating room. He was tired, hungry, and shaken.

"We saved her. We saved our Sara," he simply said. The three doctors and Nurse Lilly looked like all the blood had been drained from their faces. They looked like weary soldiers returning home from a war.

Turner said, "Let's get you all something to eat, and then you better get some sleep."

"May we see Sara?" Sister asked.

"No, not for a few days, I'm afraid. Her body, mind, and soul need to rest," Old Doc said.

"That is understandable," Turner agreed.

They all went back to Dr. Olson's house. Mr. Pepper made them something to eat. Dr. Olson offered them the two spare guest rooms. They slept for what seemed like days.

• • •

Sara opened her eyes. Was she in heaven, or did she survive that nightmare? She looked around the big room. She saw the bandages on her hands and feet. She felt the bandages on her face. She was alive, and she finally knew the truth about the fire. She could now find forgiveness in her heart for Larry. She knew what really happened that night was an accident and Larry never meant to hurt her.

• • •

Officer Danny met with Ruth and the townspeople at Precious Blood United Methodist Church. When officer Danny revealed the truth about Larry and the awful fire, some could not accept it. Some said Larry was a liar and made it up. Some found both forgiveness and compassion for Larry.

Ruth Brown found peace. The only peace a truth like that could bring.

. . .

Turner, Sister, and Old Doc rushed over to see Sara when they heard she was awake and asking for them.

Sara was sitting up in bed eating breakfast when they arrived at her hospital room.

"Oh Sara, our dear Sara," Sister Victoria said, running to Sara's bedside. "You are back. The Lord has given me my Sara back," Sister said, smiling.

"Yes, I'm back, Sister, and I am never going to leave you again," Sara said with happiness in her eyes. "Turner, you must be my guardian angel. You came to Summerville Heights and helped me to recover," Sara said, looking deep into the eyes of the man she now called brother. "I must tell you all something. You all must listen to me very carefully. I remember what happened the night of the fire," Sara proclaimed.

"Sara, you must not talk about that night. It will only bring you heartache, pain, and confusion," Old Doc said, sad and concerned.

"No, you must hear this, Doc. Please listen." Sara begged.

"Okay, we are all listening," Old Doc said.

"It was not what I thought at all. It was not Larry's fault. Larry came home late that night. I was tired, and I fell asleep with soup on the stove. Larry woke me up. The house was full of smoke already. Larry tripped and knocked over a candle. It ignited the curtains. In all the confusion and smoke, Larry, holding my hand to lead me out of the house, lost his way. The door that he thought was leading outside was really the bedroom door. The flames caught Larry's jacket on fire. His skin was burning. He still managed to break the bedroom window. He told me to jump out, but I was too afraid. Larry then passed out from the pain. When he woke up, he must have thought I jumped out, so he jumped out the window himself. When he realized I did not escape, he must have tried to come back, but when he saw everyone, he probably thought the men would string him up for setting the house ablaze. Larry was afraid and never came back to Summerville Heights."

No one quite knew what to say. Could it be true? Or was it all the stress of the last few days making Sara hallucinate? This would be not the time or the place to argue or question Sara, so for now the moment, they all agreed to give Larry the forgiveness Sara so much wanted and needed.

"Enough talk about the past. Let's talk about the future," Sister said.

"Yes, I agree," Turner said.

Then Sara asked Doc, "How long before you can remove my bandages?"

"Oh, Sara, it will be about a month," he said.

"A month. Why so long?" Sara asked.

"We have to allow your body time to heal, dear Sara." Just then, Doc Olson entered the room.

"How are you feeling today, Sara?" he said.

"To be honest, very tired," Sara replied in a sleepy voice.

"Maybe we should let Sara rest now," Turner suggested.

"Yes, let's," sister said.

"You need your rest too. We will be performing the corrective surgery the day after next," Doc Olson explained.

"Yes, we will go, and we will be back in the morning to visit with you, Sara," Sister said.

"I love you all," Sara said; then she closed her eyes and fell asleep.

• • •

"The baby is kicking," Anna said to Ruth.

"May I feel him kick?" Ruth asked politely.

"Yes, of course you can," Anna responded kindly.

Ruth eyes lit up when she felt the little angel kick. "Is John Michael getting excited about having a little brother or sister?" Ruth asked. Ruth had been staying with Forest and Anna to help Anna with John Michael and to also have company.

"John Michael is getting excited," Forest said.

• • •

Helena and Summer sat at Summer's sewing machine putting the final touches on the wedding dress.

"Oh it is beautiful. It is exactly how I dreamed it would be," Helena said, very excited.

"I'm glad you like it," Summer said.

"I'm sure Sara is going to look beautiful in the dress you made for her too. How can I ever repay you for all your kindness?" Helena asked.

"Just have a good life with Mr. Frederick," Summer replied.

• • •

"Papa, how did you know you were in love with Mama?" Little Ronnie asked his father, man to man.

"Every time I looked at your mother, my heart beat out of its chest. The moments I could not spend with her, my soul ached, but most of all, she completed my soul," he answered his son.

"Papa, can I talk to you man to man?" Little Ronnie asked sincerely.

As Ronnie looked into his son's eyes, he could see a mirror image of the look he had when he told his father he was in love with Kim. "Yes, son, you can talk to me about anything," Ronnie said sweetly.

"You like Holly Amber, right? You like her mother and father, right?" Little Ronnie asked.

"Yes, we do, son, very much. Holly is like the daughter we never had," Ronnie said.

"Papa, I think … uh … I think I am in love with Holly," Little Ronnie said passionately. "Oh, son, I am so proud and happy," Ronnie said.

"Papa, do I have yours and Mama's permission to invite Holly and her folks over for dinner so I may ask for her hand in marriage?"

"Son, of course you can," Ronnie said.

Kim, hearing everything from the kitchen, ran to her son with tears in her eyes. "Now we have to start calling you Big Ronnie," she said with a smile.

"I will always be your Little Ronnie," he replied.

• • •

Anthony Joseph had a great idea. He told Pastor about it. Pastor got the word out, and it spread to nearby towns like a wild fire.

• • •

Turner, Sister Victoria, and Old Doc discussed on the way back to the boarding house if what Sara told them about the fire was the truth.

"I guess it could be possible. They did find the bedroom window broken and a piece of burnt men's overalls on a jagged piece of broken glass from the window," Old Doc said.

"It would have been horrible if Larry had nothing to do with the fire and he spent all those years blaming himself for not being able to rescue Sara," Sister added.

"Yes, but we know if Larry didn't have anything to do with this fire, then Larry should be laid to eternal rest in Summerville Heights and not in Potter's Field," Turner said with compassion.

"Yes, but what about all those years he abused Sara?" Doc asked.

"Doc, the man spent three years rotting in a jail. Don't you think that was punishment enough?" Sister laid her heart on the line.

"I suppose you are right. If Sara could forgive, so should the people of Summerville Heights," Doc agreed. Doc composed a letter to Sara's friends to tell them about Sara's progress and about what Sara thought she remembered about the fire. He let Turner and Sister read it before he sent it out.

Chapter 12

"More lumber has just been brought in from Forest's mill," a man, not from Summerville Heights, said.

"And yes, they just delivered the furniture and clothing from Paradise Gates general store," Pastor said.

"Great. We will have to get this roof done before it rains tonight!" Forest called out from the roof to the men working on the ground.

"Please hand me those nails, Pastor," Adam said.

"Sure thing," Pastor replied.

"Mr. Frederick, how is that door frame coming?" Anthony Joseph asked.

"Almost finished," Mr. Frederick replied.

Candy Apple, Liberty, and Freedom were grazing on some grass when Old Doc and Turner elected to round them up and get them hitched to the wagon.

• • •

"Sister, are you ready?" Old Doc asked tenderly.

"I'm ready and willing." Sister giggled. She felt like a schoolgirl. Today was the day of Sister's hip surgery.

When they arrived at the hospital, Doc Friendsmore had Sister Victoria's room all ready for her.

Nurse Lilly took her into the back and got her ready.

They prayed together. The surgery would take three hours.

Turner and Old Doc went to visit Sara.

Sara was in very good spirits. "Doc Friendsmore and Doc Olson and Nurse Lilly were in to check on me earlier. They said I am recovering nicely and soon I will have my bandages taken off," Sara said excitedly. "Doc, do you think I can go outside for a bit today?" Sara asked.

"Well, if you promise you won't tire yourself out," Doc said.

Turner was excited and so relieved that Sara wanted to go outside. Turner found a wheelchair, and he and Old Doc gently lifted Sara into it.

Old Doc wheeled Sara out of her room and down a long, silent hallway to where the elevators were. The big metal doors opened to the elevator, and they stepped inside. When the elevator stopped, they found themselves in the main lobby of the hospital.

They set Sara in a little garden the hospital dedicated to all their fallen doctors. The sunlight felt good on Sara's face. Sara and Old Doc and Turner talked. Suddenly a little blue jay flew by Sara's feet.

"Oh I wish we had some bread to feed him," Sara said.

Then they heard a small, weak voice coming from behind them. "I like to feed the birds too." They turned around; behind them sat a little girl about the age of eleven. She too was a fire victim.

Sara suddenly felt that she really wasn't alone.

"How did you get burned?" the little girl asked Sara.

Sara then told her the story. The little girl then told her when she was two, she was playing with her brother and she accidentally fell on the potbelly stove. She then told Sara, Turner, and Old Doc this was her fifth surgery.

Sara felt a sisterhood with the young girl. "Were you scared during your surgery?" Sara asked.

"Whenever I get scared, I count the ladybugs and butterflies. That's why I love this place. There are always lots of ladybugs and butterflies. I like them because they can fly and be free. When I get scared, I pretend I can fly too," the little girl said. They she added, "When you get scared, you just remember those butterflies and ladybugs too."

Sara, Turner, and Old Doc were very touched on how the little girl put life in such a simple perspective.

• • •

"Ruth, I just received this letter today. It's from Old Doc," Anthony said.

"Hurry, open it," Ruth said breathlessly.

Anthony's hands were sweaty and shaky as he opened the letter. "What does it say?" Ruth asked.

Anthony read the letter. It read: "Dearest friends, Sara has had a long fight, but she is doing better. We almost lost her, but her faith in God and all your prayers have pulled her through.

"Sara has told us an incredible story of the details she remembers about the fire. She explained to us that she fell asleep with soup on the stove and that Larry did try to get her out. Larry too was burned. Sara has forgiven Larry and is now even thinking about bringing him home to Summerville Heights. Sister is no longer using a cane to walk. Turner has been talking with Sara about the past and has been helping her to heal. The other doctors and I agree that in two weeks we will take Sara's bandages off.

We all Hope to be home on Easter Sunday. Our thoughts, love, and prayers are with you all. God bless. Love Doc."

"Oh, my God, it's true. Officer Danny told us the same thing. Larry did not cause the fire!" Anthony exclaimed. Anthony was one of the people that did not believe Larry's story and could not find forgiveness. After reading Old Doc's letter, he immediately dropped to his knees and asked Ruth for her forgiveness and God for his.

Ruth then helped Anthony off the ground and said, "Anthony, we all need forgiveness and peace, and we all will help each other find it."

Anthony then embraced Ruth.

"Anthony, I love you," Ruth said.

"Ruth, I love you too," Anthony said.

"We must call for a meeting at the church to tell everyone the news," Ruth proclaimed.

"Yes, we must, but first thing I must go and check on Morning Dew, Healer, and Little Friend," Anthony explained.

"Okay, I will walk with you," Ruth said.

"I will enjoy your company," Anthony said. Anthony and Ruth, although they were courting, had not been able to be alone together in quite a long time.

• • •

Holly Amber went to her dresses and picked out the prettiest one to wear to the Miller farm. She seemed to know that tonight would be different from all the other dates she had had with Little Ronnie. It started to rain, but even the rain would not ruin tonight.

Adam had just gotten back from his blacksmith shop when Little Ronnie extended the invitation. Adam was very fond of Little Ronnie and his family. In his heart, he knew Little Ronnie would make a fine husband for Holly.

Summer knew that tonight was her daughter's big night. She told her daughter she could borrow her mother's pearl necklace to wear this evening. Holly was excited.

Kim and Ronnie were getting ready for the big evening too.

"Should I wear my blue suit or gray one?" Ronnie asked Kim.

"The blue one. It brings out the color of your eyes," Kim answered.

"I wonder if Mr. Frederick would like to borrow my gray one to wear tonight then." Ronnie said.

"Why don't you ask him? I'm sure he would appreciate the offer," Kim said.

"I shall do that after I get dressed."

Little Ronnie had asked his father earlier if he could go out and pick some flowers for his mama, Holly, and Summer. His father told him to go right ahead. Little Ronnie had gone to his favorite place to pick the flowers. It was beside the little stream that ran through town. Pretty wild flowers always grew there. He picked some wild roses, sweet Williams, lilies, and baby's breath. He made three small pretty bunches to give to his three favorite ladies that evening at dinner.

• • •

When Forest came home for supper, he was wet, tired, cold and hungry. He and the other men from the mill, Gingerbread Landing, Paradise Gates, and from town had been working on Sara's surprise for nearly a month now. Every night at supper he would tell his wife and John about the progress they had made on it. Tonight when he came home, he told Anna it was finally finished.

Anna was overcome by pure joy. "This will be the best gift ever for Sara."

Pastor Peter, who had just come home for supper, told Amy Carrie the glorious news. He and Amy then prayed for the other men who helped make it all possible.

• • •

Anthony and Ruth walked together over to the pastor's house to tell them about the letter from Old Doc. When they knocked on the door, they were greeted by Amy's warm smile. "Do come in," Amy said.

"But we don't want to disturb your supper," Ruth said.

"Come in, come in; don't be silly," Pastor called from behind the door.

"Why, thank you," Anthony said. They then told Pastor and Amy about the letter.

Pastor then said, "In our own human skin, we often make mistakes as Larry did, but in God's grace we are forgiven."

"Yes, Pastor, you are right," Anthony said. They broke bread together and talked about what would be best for the town next. Pastor also told them that Sara's surprise was finished.

"Wonderful," Ruth said.

"God is sure showing his favor on us isn't he?" Anthony added.

"He sure is," Amy said.

"Life will change for Sara, and us too," Pastor said.

"Yes, but it's an exciting change," Amy added.

"It sure will be. I can't wait till Sara sees herself the way we always saw her: beautiful," Ruth said.

"Yes, she certainly will see how much we love her when she comes home," Anthony said.

• • •

"Oh, Mama, the rain has stopped," Holly said cheerfully.

"I'm glad. I did not want the pretty curls in your hair to drop," Summer said to her daughter.

"Excuse me, ladies, I do not want to interrupt your beauty talk, but it's nearly six. Honey, are you ready for your big night?" Adam said.

"Yes, Pop, I have been waiting for this for a long time," Holly said in a nervous voice.

Adam helped his daughter and wife into their wagon that was pulled by their horses, Snowflake and Raindrop. On their drive, they noticed how beautiful Sara's gift was. Happiness Trail was full of God's work. Wild flowers strung against new green grass, tress kissed the sky, grass-hoppers were hopping, and crickets were singing their beautiful soulful melodies. Holly looked around at all the beautiful things God placed on his earth. She whispered this prayer to herself: "Thank you, God, for giving me eyes to see the beauty of your trees and flowers, for giving me the perfume of honey suckle and jasmine. Thank you, God for the perfection of your handiwork."

"We are almost at the Miller farm, Holly," Summer announced.

• • •

Kim was setting the table when Little Ronnie walked into the kitchen.

"My God, son, you look just like your father did the night he proposed to me. Come over here by the candle-light so I can see you better," Kim said.

"Son, I have something for you. This is the handker-chief I wore in my pocket the night I proposed to your mother. I want you to have it," Ronnie said to his son with a look of pride.

"But, Pa, I can't take this," Little Ronnie said.

"Son, it belongs to you now. Your granddad gave it to me, and now I give it to you."

"Thank you. I love you," Little Ronnie said.

"I love you too, son," Ronnie said, all choked up.

Just then Mr. Frederick and Helena walked in. Mr. Frederick looked like a proud adoring uncle. "If you shall get engaged tonight, we will have a double wedding."

"Wouldn't that be wonderful?" Helena asked.

"You look good in the gray suit," Ronnie said.

"Thank you for letting me borrow it," Mr. Freder-ick said. Before they could say anything else, there was a knock on the door.

"How do I look?" Little Ronnie asked.

"Perfect," Mr. Frederick said. Little Ronnie ran to the door, excited, thinking it was Holly and her parents, but it was Ruth and Anthony.

"We are sorry to disturb you at this late hour, but we are so glad you are here," Anthony said. He then told them about Old Doc's letter. They rejoiced in the news. Kim extended an invitation for dinner, but they declined.

Chapter 13

Pastor stopped at Forest's and Anna's after dinner to tell them the news of Sara. Pastor and Amy joined Forest and Anna in sharing a slice of homemade apple pie.

Mr. Frederick answered the door when Holly and her parents came to the Miller farm. Holly was dressed in a cream-colored linen dress, around her shoulders was a white crocheted shawl, and around her neck was her mother's pearl necklace. She had some light blush on.

"Hello, and good evening," Little Ronnie said. "Mrs. Tinner, these are for you, and, Holly, these are for you," Little Ronnie said, handing them the picked flowers he got earlier.

"How sweet," Summer said. "Thank you."

He then walked over to Mr. Tinner and firmly shook his hand.

"Good strong handshake. I like that in a young man," Mr. Tinner said. Ronnie then invited them in, and they all took seats around the table.

"Mrs. Miller, may I help you with anything?" Holly asked sweetly.

"No, darling, you just sit and enjoy yourself," Kim responded.

Mr. Frederick, Adam, Ronnie, and Little Ronnie made

small talk about hunting, fishing, and woodwork. Summer, Holly, Helena, and Kim talked about the upcoming wedding. Holly had a lump in her throat thinking she may be the next lady in town to be planning a wedding.

Kim laid a beautiful pig roast on the table. It lay on a silver tray and was garnished with carrots, sliced apples, and cherry tomatoes. Alongside the roast was a bowl full of mashed potatoes and another bowl with collard greens, another with okra, and then corn bread.

"You must have gone through a lot of trouble to fix this for us," Summer said.

"Thank you for your kind hospitality," said Adam.

Kim smiled at them and gave Summer a wink. "We are practically family, and only the best for family."

Ronnie cleared his throat. He made a toast to the happy occasion and said grace. The prayer he prayed was a happy one. Adam added to the prayer. Looking straight at Little Ronnie, he said, "'But for Adam no suitable helper was found. So the LORD God caused the man to fall into a deep sleep; and while he was sleeping, he took out one of the man's ribs and closed the place with flesh. Then the LORD God made a woman from the rib... For this reason a man will leave his mother his father and be united with his wife, and the two shall become one flesh.' Genesis 2:20–24."

After Adam had said that, Little Ronnie said, "Excuse me, Pa, Ma, and friends, after we eat, I must talk with Mr. Tinner. Pa, and Holly, okay?" They all agreed.

They enjoyed Kim's home cooked meal. The women cleared the table. Adam, Ronnie, Holly, and Little Ronnie walked into the parlor to talk. Little Ronnie said, "Mr. Tinner, I love your daughter with all my heart and soul.

When I'm not with her, I cannot breathe. I am asking you, before God and my father, if I may have Holly's hand in marriage?"

Adam took a moment to say, "Little Ronnie, I am very fond of you and your family. If you promise to treat Holly as the heavenly daughter she is, you have her mother's and my blessing."

"Oh, Pa, I love you!" Holly said, running to her father and embracing him. The four of them showed no emotion as they walked back into the kitchen. Kim had a sinking feeling in her gut until Holly said, "Ma, you will have another order for a wedding dress soon!"

Everyone let out a noise of cheerful voices, and a new extended family was born under the celebration of heaven. Ronnie also filled in his family about Sara's memory of the fire.

• • •

"Sara, I am slowly going to start unwrapping your bandages," Old Doc said. Sister and Turner held on to each other. Slowly Old Doc unwrapped the brown bandage from Sara's left hand. Sara, too scared to look, kept her eyes shut. Dr. Friendsmore and Dr. Olson were quite impressed on how quickly Sara healed. Old Doc stood in awe of Sara's creamy white skin.

"Turner, look, look," Sister whispered.

"I see God's miracle," he whispered back.

"Don't you want to take a look, Sara?" Old Doc asked.

"I am not ready yet," Sara replied.

Old Doc learned a long time ago Sara did things in

her own timing. He did not push her. He then unwrapped her right hand, her legs, and finally her radiant face.

"Sara, you look like an angel," Sister said.

"Turner, how do I really look?" Sara asked. She had put much weight on Turner's opinion and advice. She had grown a deep friendship with him.

"You look like you have just fallen from heaven," Turner said so sweetly.

"Sara, do you want to be alone when you look in the mirror?" Doc Friendsmore asked.

"Yes, I think so," Sara replied slowly.

Sara then heard the kind voice of Nurse Lilly. "Sara, I want you to keep this mirror when you go home. Whenever you look at it and see your beautiful reflection, I want you to remember how much we all love you."

Sara, still not opening her eyes, reached out for Nurse Lilly to give her a hug.

"The mirror is beside you on the right," Nurse Lilly said. "We are all going to be right outside your door if you need us," Turner said. "

"Thank you all," Sara said. She was so afraid to open her eyes; then she remembered what that little girl told her in the park. She pictured herself as a butterfly coming out of her cocoon. Then the voice of Grandpa Miller echoed in her head. *He will give you beauty for your ashes.* A wave of courage came over her. She picked up the mirror and opened her eyes. For the first time since the fire she did not scream at her own image.

"It is really me," Sara said. Sara still had a burn mark on the right cheek of her face and also the skin on her left ear, but she did not look anything like she did before the surgery."

"My God, my God, thank you! Thank you!" was all Sara was able to say.

Her friends heard her and went back into the room. Crying, they all joined hands. They praised God for his miracle. Sister Victoria quoted from Songs of Songs: "How beautiful your sandaled feet, oh princess daughter, your graceful legs are like jewels, the work of craftsman hands, your naval is like a round goblet that never lacked blended wine, your waist is a mound of wheat encircled by lilies. Your breath are like two fawns twins of gazelle, your neck is like an ivy tower, your eyes are like the Pools of Heshnon by the Gates of Bath Rabbin, your head crowns you like Mount Carmal, how beautiful you are and how pleasing."

"Sister, you embarrass me," Sara said.

"Sara, you have to learn how to take a compliment now. You are going to be getting plenty of them," Sister said.

"When can I go home?" Sara asked.

"Day after tomorrow," Doc Olson said with a hint of sadness in his voice.

"Don't worry, Doc. I will never forget you. Doc Friendsmore and Nurse Lilly, your faces are now branded on my heart; we are friends for life."

"We will all come visit you at the wedding. We want to see you dance," Nurse Lilly said.

"Oh, you will. That is a promise." Sara smiled.

• • •

The town was abuzz with happiness and gladness. News of Holly and Little Ronnie's engagement was on everyone's lips. They all waited for the return of Sara, Turner, Sister, and Old Doc.

Anna's due date was drawing closer. Pastor and Amy had just finished putting on the extension of their church. Mr. Frederick and Helena's wedding plans were nearly complete. And tomorrow was resurrection Sunday.

• • •

Sara went to go say goodbye to the little girl next to her——the girl who taught her so much about courage, strength, and bravery. When Sara went to go see her, she was not there. Sara wondered where she was.

Sara saw Nurse Lilly in the hallway, so she asked her. "Sara, I'm afraid that her surgery was not as successful as yours. She went home to the Lord last night."

Sara broke down. Nurse Lilly took her hand and said, "Sara, she can be like a free butterfly now. Would you like to take a walk with me to her garden?"

"Yes, I would like that," Sara said.

As they sat and talked on the little girl's favorite bench in the park, Sara asked, "What was the little girl's name? I never asked her."

Nurse Lilly answered, "Hope."

Just as she answered Sara's question, a little yellow butterfly flew between them and landed on Sara's leg. "Yes, that name suited her. Hope," Sara said. She looked down at the butterfly and said, "Goodbye, Hope."

Just then they were greeted by Turner, Old Doc, and Sister. "Sara, are you ready to go home?" Sister asked.

"Yes, I am," Sara answered. "I now have hope." Sara said goodbye to Nurse Lilly. Then they went to Dr. Friendsmore's office and said goodbye to him. Dr. Friendsmore gave Sara a gift. It was a basket of yellow flowers.

"Sara, my mom always loved yellow flowers, so that's why I'm giving these to you."

The four friends went to go say goodbye to Dr. Olson, Mr. Pepper, and Mr. Miles last. They all wished their friends a trip home full of God's protection. They all promised to keep in touch and see each other again.

On the way back to Summerville Heights, Sara took in all the pretty sights and smells of spring. "Sara, how do you feel?" Old Doc kept asking her like a concerned father.

"I feel wonderful, Doc, just wonderful," Sara replied. "Turner, could you please stop here a moment, near that old oak tree?"

Turner did as Sara requested. "Sara, are you sick?" Sister asked with worry in her voice.

"No, Sister, not at all," Sara said cheerfully. Sara then told her friends about the secret picnic she had with her father every summer.

"You miss that, don't you, Sara?" Turner asked tenderly.

"Yes, brother, I do so much," Sara answered.

"Well, Sara, we can't bring your father back, but we can sure have a special picnic," Turner said.

"What a great idea," Sister said.

"We have that nice basket Mr. Pepper packed for us," Sara said. Old Doc took out a blanket and spread it under the old mighty oak tree. Turner then helped Sister and Sara out of the wagon. They sat under the shaded branches of the oak. Turner then got out the pretty wicker basket Mr. Pepper had given them. When Turner opened the lid, he found four plates, four knives, four forks, and four drinking glasses. The four friends then smelled the sweet aroma of fried chicken, cob corn, apple pie, fresh peaches, and sweet tea. "Mr. Pepper sure makes a mighty good meal," Old Doc said.

Turner then said a blessing. Sara found much joy in the simple pleasure of having a picnic with her friends. She enjoyed the parade of the marching ants, hearing the birds sing their sweet lullaby, and the warmth of the sun. After they were done eating, Sara ran barefoot across the grass. Something she hadn't done since she was a little girl.

Turner was very much moved watching Sara find joy in God's every day little miracles. Old Doc and Sister found great unspeakable happiness.

• • •

The whole town was dressed in their Sunday best. Today was no ordinary Sunday. It was resurrection Sunday. Although they were very excited about today, they were a little disappointed that Sara, Doc, Turner, and Sister were not able to join them for Easter service.

"This is the day of the Lord," Pastor Peter said from his pulpit. "Let us praise God's goodness," he went on to say. He then read the story of Jesus resurrection from the Bible.

"Jesus died so we may live. Jesus died so we may know love," said a familiar voice from the back of the church. Everyone almost got whiplash from spinning their heads around so fast. It was Turner, Old Doc, and Sister, but Sara was not with them.

"Welcome home." Pastor ran to them so fast, he almost tripped on his own shoelaces.

"Welcome home, brother." Mr. Frederick also ran to Turner.

"Please, everyone, take your seats please," Old Doc announced.

"We need to talk," Turner said. Tears of joy suddenly turned into frightened faces.

"No, please don't fret," Sister said.

"The new Sara has requested we all be seated for her grand entrance. Sara has also asked that until she has finished speaking that everyone hold off on asking her any questions," Old Doc announced. "Sara would like everyone's undivided attention." The church went silent.

The big doors swung open and a beautiful vision stepped inside. Sara was wearing a crisp, white, linen dress. She had pretty stockings on, white high-heel shoes, and a white lily nestled behind her right ear. Everyone looked at beautiful Sara. Helena cried. Kim sucked in her breath. Summer and Holly, never seeing Sara before, thought she looked like a messenger from heaven. Everyone respected Sara's wishes and dared not speak before she finished speaking.

Sara walked up to Pastor Peter's pulpit and embraced him. She then asked if she might address his congregation. Pastor was so overcome by joy, all he could do was nod his head yes.

Sara, with a tremble in her voice, looked out at all her beloved friends and some new faces too. She said, "I love you all. You have given me my life back." She then quoted Job 11:13. "Yet if you devote your heart to him and stretch out your hands to him, if you put away the sin that's in your hand and allow no evil to dwell in your tent, then you will lift up your faith without shame; you will stand firm and without fear. You will surely forget your trouble, recalling it only as waters gone by. Life will be brighter than noon-day and darkness will become like the morning. You will be secure, because there is Hope; you will look about you and take your rest in his safety. You will lie down, with no one to make you afraid, and many will count your favor." Sara went on to say, "My dear, dear friends, you believed in me even when I forgot how to believe in myself. You loved me when I thought I was unlovable. You showed me God's grace even when I thought I was not worthy. You gave me forgiveness so I may forgive another. You gave me strength when I was weak. You carried me through my dark days and made me see heaven's light again. How can I ever repay you for showing me that God still cared?"

Helena then walked with shaky legs up to Sara. "Sara, some day give love to someone who thinks they're unlov-able. Believe in someone who forgot to believe in them-selves. Share with someone God's grace who thinks there never worthy of it."

"Oh, Helena, my dear sweet sister. I've missed you." Sara wrapped her arms around her friend.

Ruth then greeted Sara. Sara, with a look of genuine love, said, "I want to bring Larry home." Ruth almost col-lapsed at hearing the words come out of Sara's mouth. "I remember the truth." Sara shared it with everyone.

Kim was amazed and moved. She then shared with Sara that she saw a vision of Grandpa Miller and Larry together.

One by one they welcomed Sara home. Today was not only the Lord's resurrection day, but Sara's too. Sara then said, "Friends, I have told you the truth about Larry. I want to bring him home." Everyone agreed it was time to forgive Larry. They were going to bring him home.

Ruth then told Sara about Officer Danny. "Officer Danny said Larry never ever stopped loving her. Larry turned himself in to the law because he said you changed his heart, and he found Jesus because of your great love and forgiveness you showed him through his drinking years."

"You mean Larry did love me?" Sara asked.

"Yes, he always did," Ruth answered.

"We must bring Larry home then," Sara said with love in her voice.

Pastor then said, "Sara, may I close with a prayer?" He prayed simply, "Love never fails. Dear Lord, thank you for loving us." All responded "Amen" to Pastor's simple, heartfelt prayer.

They all walked over to the fellowship hall. Sara and Helena walked arm and arm, so wanting to let go of each other. When they got to the fellowship hall, Sara caught up on all the gossip going on around town. She noticed the new addition to the church and found out Anna was expecting again and that Little Ronnie was now engaged. Sara also learned that Holly had great ambition to be a dancer. Sara held for the first time baby John Michael. He immediately took to Sara. Sara immediately was lifted of the void of losing her own child.

Sara visited with her friends for a while, and then Sara started getting tired. She asked Turner to take her home. Turner talked with Sara for a while to stall her so the rest of the town could race to her home to see Sara's face when her surprise was revealed.

• • •

The moon glowing through the trees made it look like the tree branches were dancing. As Sara and Turner rode

Morning Dew, it was almost like her loving animal could pick up on her happiness.

Sara's little house sat behind an orchard and peach farm, so she was not able to see her house through the trees. She could not see her friends waiting to see Sara's expression. As Morning Dew galloped down the dirt road leading to her house, her friends called out, "Welcome home!"

Chapter 14

In front of Sara's eyes was a vision right out of one of her daydreams. She first noticed the beautiful garden that was planted near her parents' graves. In the garden there were red roses, yellow iris, pink carnations, a lilac bush, and hundreds of butterflies.

"It is just like the one Mama had." Sara cried.

"Yes, Sara. Now you can give your mother a fresh flower every day from your garden,"

Helena said. In front of her kitchen window was planted a weeping willow tree. "Sara, this is to remind you that God will give you beauty for your ashes," Pastor said.

"Oh, it's so beautiful," Sara proclaimed. Next Sara saw the wrap-around porch that was rebuilt on her house. It brought back memories of her mother and father sitting on it in their rocking chairs. On the porch there was also a wooden swing Forest had built with his own two hands.

Sara could almost not bring herself to walk up the stairs and to open the door to her new rebuilt home. As she got to the front door, she noticed a sign hanging above it that Mr. Frederick had made. It read, "As for me and my house, we shall serve the Lord."

Sara's shaking hand turned the brass doorknob on the front door. When she swung it open, Sara was encircled with a feeling of belonging, warmth, and love. She stepped inside with all of her friends trailing behind her. Her petite feet stepped on a bearskin rug. The first bear Little Ronnie had ever shot.

"We wanted you to have it to remind you that you have the strength of a bear," Little Ronnie said.

As she looked around the room, she saw a stone fireplace. Hanging above it was a hundred-year-old mantle. It had belonged to Grandpa Miller. She saw her beloved rocking chair and her mother's teacups. Sara's eyes went wide when she saw a brand new cedar Hope chest. It was engraved with hearts, and the inscription read: "Sara, love never fails." Sara raced to it, and like a child unwrapping a Christmas gift, lifted the lid. Inside of it was a flowing gown and beautiful glass slippers.

"For you to wear at our wedding," Helena said.

Sara didn't know where to look first. In her living room, the men made her a bay window. In her bedroom that was painted a pale pink, Sara found new clothes and a new brass four-post bed.

"Sara, come outside behind the house," Turner said.

Sara went outside. Behind her house the men built a new stable for Morning Dew.

"How did you ... When did you ... Where did you get all the money to do this?" Sara asked.

Summer explained. "Sara, Pastor and Anthony put a call out to all that could help. Men came from all over, as far away as Paradise Gates. That's what brought us here Sara. My husband is a blacksmith, and I, a seamstress. We heard from our pastor about you, and we came here to help. We fell in love with Summerville Heights, so we stayed."

Turner then said, giving a wink to Adam, "Remember when I first came here I told you about my journey and the kind family I met who fed me and clothed me? Well, Adam, Summer, and Holly were the family that I was talking about."

Adam then shook hands with Turner and said, "We never knew if our paths would cross again, but under the stars of heaven, God made us meet once more." Everyone was amazed on how God was setting his plan in motion.

"Sara, you look very tired," Anthony said. She was. All of Sara's friends said good night. Helena tucked Sara into her new bed. Sara sunk down deep into its comfort and warmth and fell fast asleep. Helena took one of Sara's new throws and settled into the rocking chair for the night.

When Sara awoke to a golden sunrise the next morning, she was not sure if all of it was a dream. She looked into the little hand-held mirror Nurse Lilly had given her and saw her radiant reflection smiling back. "God, you are always an incredible, generous God. What can I do to show my thanks?" Sara whispered.

"Well, good morning sleepy head. I fixed you some breakfast," Helena said.

"Thank you, Helena," Sara replied.

"How are you feeling today?" Helena asked with all the concern of a sister.

"Glorious," Sara replied.

"Why don't we open these curtains and let some of the sun in?" Helena said.

"Yes, be my guest, I don't want to hide in darkness anymore. Each new morning holds new promise and meaning for me now," Sara said.

"Speaking of new promise, we must discuss the wedding," Sara said happily to Helena.

"Yes, but first we will eat. I have laid out fresh towels, hot water, and a clean dress for you. Do you need help?" Helena asked, concerned.

"Thanks, sister. I can manage. Please don't fuss over me. I love you for your concern, but I am healed enough to manage," Sara replied.

"Okay, then I will fix your plate while you bathe and dress," Helena said, leaving Sara alone.

Sara looked around the room, still in awe of the beauty and painstaking craftsmanship. Sara got washed and dressed. She then joined Helena for breakfast. Sara told Helena about the little girl she met at the hospital and all her new friends. Helena listened, riveted to her story. The two friends then discussed Helena wedding plans.

● ● ●

"Well, where did you come from, little guy? Little Ronnie asked. *Woof, woof,* the little black and white dog barked. "I have got to find Papa and tell him about you. Papa, I was milking Little Honey, and this puppy came out of nowhere," Little Ronnie told his father.

"Don't know anyone around here who has a dog, but we will keep him until we find his owner," Ronnie said. Ronnie then directed his son to give the puppy some food and water. Little Ronnie did.

Just then Mr. Frederick came into the house. "Whose puppy?" he asked.

"Don't know; he just came from nowhere," Ronnie explained.

"What are we going to call him?" Mr. Frederick asked.

"How about Joy? His tail wagging sure makes him look like one little bundle of joy," Little Ronnie said.

"Joy it is then," Mr. Frederick said.

• • •

Ruth got to her ice cream parlor early for her Monday's delivery. As she sat in her favorite chair behind the register, she thought about all the happiness God had given her and this town. She thought about the day she would be able to lay Larry to rest in Summerville Heights, and she thought about her future.

• • •

"Oh, Mom, it will be perfect," Holly Amber said as she sat with her mother over her Singer sewing machine designing her wedding gown.

"Honey, I want you to have my veil, and I want you to use your grandmother's wedding shoes," Summer said.

"It will be my honor, Mom. Do you think I should ask Sister Victoria and Ruth to be my witnesses?" Holly asked thoughtfully.

"That would be a very kind thing to do. If we are going to do that, then we must find out what color dresses they want to wear," Summer said.

"Yes, Mom. I will find out on Sunday," Holly responded.

• • •

"John Michael, are you hungry?" Anna asked her growing boy.

"Belly hungry," he responded.

"Papa will be home soon for lunch so we will be eating soon," Anna said patiently to her son.

• • •

Anthony Joseph had plenty of orders to fill at the general store today. He worked all morning to pack and fill orders. He then took a break to have lunch with Ruth.

"It's a pretty day outside today," Ruth said to him.

"It sure is. We should have a picnic," Anthony said with a huge smile. Ruth took him up on his offer. During lunch, Ruth and Anthony talked about Sara and about bringing Larry home.

• • •

"Turner and Old Doc are here, Sara," Helena called into her bedroom where Sara went to rest after her breakfast.

"May we come in?" Old Doc asked.

"Yes, of course," Sara responded.

"How are you feeling today, my dear"? Old Doc asked.

"Fine, I am a little tired, but feeling wonderful otherwise," Sara said honestly.

"Sara, I don't want you to overdo it. I know you want to see all your friends, but you still must rest," Doc said with genuine concern in his voice.

"Okay, Doc," Sara, promised. "I am glad you are here though. I need to talk to you both about something. Helena, would you join us too?" Sara asked. Helena walked over to her bedside. "I am going to ask Ruth to come live with me, "Sara said matter-of-factly. "I need her, and she needs me, and we are family," Sara went on.

Helena said, "Your concern for Ruth is very noble, but she and Anthony are courting. Do you think she will move in with you?"

"I did not know she and Anthony were courting. Are they in love?" Sara said.

"We believe so. They have shown a great commitment to each other," Old Doc revealed.

"I am glad Ruth has got Anthony. I do not want her to be alone in this world," Sara said with a look of relief.

"Sara, if you are worried about staying here alone, I shall stay as long as you need me," Helena said.

"Helena, you are sweet to offer, but you have your own wedding to plan; besides, I know Doc and Turner will check in on me," Sara said sweetly.

"Hello, may I come in?" asked the voice of Sister Victoria.

"Do come in, please," Sara responded.

"Sara, I made sandwiches, but I see you have a lot of company. I'm assuming you ate already?" Sister said.

"Yes, Sister, but I am glad you are here," Sara said.

Helena then had a bright idea. "Sister, we were discussing about who would stay with Sara during her recovery," Helena revealed.

"Say no more. I will go home and pack," Sister said with a wide-toothed smile.

"Oh, thank you! If you all don't mind, I'd like for us to go out and sit in the garden, I want to see all my beautiful flowers under the full sunlight," Sara said.

Turner helped Sara out of bed, and they all went to Sara's garden. Last night, in all of the beautiful chaos, Sara was not able to see all her plants. In her garden, there was a beautiful hand-painted ceramic angel statue, a water pond, and some exotic plants.

• • •

"Forest, it is time. You need to get Old Doc. The baby is coming," Anna said in a calm, smooth voice. Forest met Mr. Frederick on Happiness Trail and told him the news.

"I will gather our friends. You go get Old Doc," Mr. Frederick said.

It was a hot summer day. The birds were chirping as Mr. Frederick gathered Anna's friends for the arrival of the new baby.

Forest found Old Doc, Sister, Turner, and Helena at Sara's house. This time even Sara insisted on being present for the birth.

"Too bad Pastor and Amy aren't here, but they will be with us in spirit," Mr. Frederick said.

The men were waiting outside the stable praying while the women of the town helped in assisting of the birth. Sara was the lead midwife for this birth.

Inside the small room were Summer, Holly, Sara, Sister, Ruth, Kim, Helena, and Old Doc. Holly, who had never seen a woman give birth, was both fascinated and taken back.

"What can I do to help, Mom?" Holly asked.

"Just pray, darling," Anna said with a voice weakened by labor pains. Sara fixed herbal tea to help with the pain. She also rubbed her legs and arms. Sister Victoria heated a washcloth and placed it on Anna's back to help with pain. Old Doc had a very surprised look on his face.

He whispered to Sara, "Sisters."

"Twins," Sara whispered back.

"Yes." Old Doc eyed his aids.

"Push, sweetheart, push," Old Doc cheered on.

Anna was exhausted. She had been in labor for hours now. Ruth kept the men informed of the birth, but only Sara and Old Doc knew of the miracle to come.

"Doc, I can't. I am so tired." Anna cried.

"Honey, you have to," Sara cheered. "It's a girl," Doc said.

"Oh God, oh God! Pain—why hasn't the pain stopped?" Anna cried out.

"Push," Sara said.

"I can't. I . . . I, hurt!" Anna cried.

"Push, Anna, push," Old Doc said.

"I have to stop!" Anna cried even harder.

"Push, Anna, push; you are having twins," Old Doc said.

The women in the room kept encouraging Anna.

"It's another girl," Sara said with tears streaming down her cheeks.

"Two daughters. I have two daughters!" Anna shouted with joy. "Let me see my babies," Anna said.

Ruth went out to tell the men. "Shout to the Lord thanksgiving and praise," Forest said. "I have two daughters!"

The men congratulated Forest. Then Forest ran to his wife and new baby girls.

One of the babies had curly blond hair and bright blue eyes; the other baby had wavy brown hair and brown eyes.

"Are they healthy, Doc?" Forest asked nervously.

"Yes, yes," Doc declared.

"What shall we name them?" Anna asked. They both looked at Sara. Anna said, "We shall call the baby with the brown hair Sara Faith and the other baby Amanda Grace."

Sara was overwhelmed by Anna's gesture. Sara took

Anna by the hand and said, "Anna, you have just given me faith."

Ruth then said, "The men would like to come in to see the babies, and John Michael would like to meet his sisters. Shall I send everyone in?" Sister Victoria first insisted on cleaning up Anna and the babies.

Standing shoulder to shoulder in the small bedroom, everyone in town was there to admire the new babies. Turner then led everyone in prayer.

Just then Pastor Peter and Amy entered the room refreshed from the pastor's meeting. Pastor added to Turner's prayer with Scripture from the book of Genesis. "I will surely bless you and make your descendents as numerous as the stars in the sky and the sands in the sea shore." As Pastor was praying, Anna exhausted body gave into sleep. Quietly everyone left the room one by one. Kim stayed to help.

Turner took Sara and Sister home. On the way back to Sara's house, they all saw a shooting star. Sister quietly prayed, Sara made a wish, and Turner took in its beauty.

"Did you see that?" Sara questioned.

"Sure did," Turner said.

"It was God smiling down on us," Sister said.

When they got back to Sara's house, Sara told Turner he may sleep in the rocking chair in the living room because it was so late.

Turner said to Sara, "I appreciate the offer, but I must help with Mr. Frederick tomorrow with the stables, so I must get home tonight."

Sara then said, "Thank you, Turner, for taking us home." Turner then left.

Sara slipped into her bedclothes, and so did sister. They retired to the big queen-size bed for the night. Everyone rested peacefully in Summerville Heights that night.

Chapter 15

The next morning Turner was up bright and early to help Mr. Frederick. They cleaned the stables, milked the cows, and collected eggs.

Ronnie and Little Ronnie went to the general store to make a delivery. When they arrived at the store, they found Anthony talking to Ruth.

"Good morning, gentlemen," Ruth said.

"Good morning," they replied.

"Ruth and I were just discussing the wedding plans. We were also talking about how happy you and Holly will be," Anthony said.

"I know. Holly Amber will make a great wife," Little Ronnie said, blushing.

"Do you know the date your wedding will be yet?" Ruth inquired.

"Yes, it will be on Holly's birthday, August 20," Little Ronnie replied. A happy air of glee fell between the friends.

• • •

"Baby, baby, my baby," John said, looking down at his tiny little sisters.

"Yes, your new sisters," Forest said lovingly to his son.

"Baby hungry, Daddy," John Michael said.

"Yes, babies eat a lot and sleep a lot too," Anna explained to her son.

Sara Faith was wrapped in a little pink blanket. She was longer and weighed a little bit more than Amanda Grace. Sara cried a hungry cry while Amanda lay peacefully, dreaming. Amanda was wrapped in a little white blanket.

John Michael curiously watched as Anna fed Sara and then woke Amanda to feed her too.

"Is big brother hungry?" Kim asked John Michael.

"John, Miss Kim will fix you a little breakfast," Anna announced.

"Eat, Mommy," John Michael said.

"Yes, you go eat, John Michael," Forest directed.

Kim picked up John Michael in her arms and brought him to the kitchen. She fixed him peanut butter on crackers and gave him some milk. The little tyke ate very fast because he did not want to miss a moment with his new baby sisters.

• • •

Old Doc saddled up Healer and rode him over to Sara's house. When he arrived at Sara's doorstep, he found Sara and Sister talking over sweet tea and cookies. Sara had nice red color in her cheeks, and her hair was growing longer. Old Doc was very pleased with her recovery.

"Come join us. I made sweet tea and butter cookies," Sara said pleasantly.

"Don't mind if I do," Old Doc replied.

"Sara and I were just talking about writing a letter to Officer Danny to ask him to bring Larry home," Sister said.

"Yes, but I want to talk about it with Ruth first before we do. I also want to talk to everyone on Sunday after Sara and Amanda's christening," Sara said.

"Good, I think that would be best," Old Doc said.

. . .

Summer, Adam, Helena, Mr. Frederick, Little Ronnie, Holly, and Ronnie were going over last minute details about the wedding at the Millers' kitchen table. Kim had just arrived home.

"We can have a pretty picture taken right over there at the pond," Kim said.

"Yes, we can also dress the weeping willow trees with white crepe paper and have them in the background," Summer added.

"It is going to be the perfect double wedding." Mr. Frederick smiled.

"I can't believe it will be here in less than three weeks," Holly said with thrilled eyes.

"I sure Hope Nurse Lilly, Dr. Olson, Dr. Friendsmore, and Mr. Pepper will be able to come," Little Ronnie added.

. . .

Pastor Peter and Amy sat in their back yard under the shaded arms of a large oak tree.

"Can you believe all the goodness and miracles God has performed here in the last few weeks?" Pastor said to Amy.

"God, slow to anger and always quick to show love, has given us a great many blessings in the past few weeks," Amy replied.

Mr. Pepper opened the door to the big wooden mailbox in front of Doc Olson's house. "A wedding invitation," Doc said. Doc Friendsmore and Nurse Lilly had already gotten theirs.

"We are going to see our dear friend, Sara, soon, Mr. Pepper," Doc said with a joyful voice. Mr. Pepper responded with a wide smile.

Nurse Lilly picked out her prettiest dress to wear to the wedding. She also picked up, from Paradise Gates general store, a beautiful set of towels as wedding gifts.

Dr. Friendsmore was very excited to go to the wedding. He thought to himself, *I will finally get that dance. Sara owes me. I Hope she is fully recovered by now.*

• • •

It was Sunday morning, and the summer sun was burning with the color of bright orange and yellow. Everyone in town was dressed to the tee for Amanda and Sara's christening day.

Forest held Amanda close to his heart. Baby Amanda was wearing a little pink ruffled dress with panties to match. Around her tiny neck was a cross. John had a tiny gray pinstriped suit on. He was sitting next to Forest. Anna held baby Sara. Cradling Sara in her arms, Anna could feel her hot baby breath blowing against her cheek. Sara was wearing a white dress with pink lace. Also around her neck was a cross. One by one, Amanda's friends and Sara's friends came to adore the little girls in the new outfits.

Pastor Peter welcomed his congregation and then began to pray. He prayed, "Jesus answered, "I tell you the truth, no one can enter the kingdom of God unless he is born of water and the Spirit. Flesh gives birth to flesh, but the Spirit gives birth to the spirit. John 3:5.'"

Pastor Peter then asked Anna, Forest, and Sara, who was chosen to be the babies' Godmother, and Turner, chosen to be the babies' Godfather, to come to the altar. As Pastor Peter poured water over the little babies' heads, he said, "Lord, send out your Spirit upon these children; make then wise in your ways." He then dried the babies' heads. Sara and Turner were then directed to light a white candle. Together they lit the candle. Then Pastor Peter, looking down at the beautiful babies, said, "Like a candle in the darkness, may you always be an example of Christ's love. I baptize you in the name of the Father, Son, and Holy Ghost."

Pastor then asked everyone to join hands. They prayed the Our Father. After they got done praying, the normally quiet church broke out into loud applause.

Pastor Peter and Turner were the first to congratulate them. After the heart-tugging service, everyone walked along the dirt path leading to the fellowship hall.

The new addition that Pastor had added on to the hall was all dressed for the special occasion. There were two round tables covered with white tablecloths with pink trim. On the table sat flowers donated from both Kim and Sara's gardens. Each chair had a name card for the guest. Around the room were balloons and paper decorations. On a long wooden table that was covered with a pink tablecloth were delicious, mouth-watering treats Helena had made. There were fruit pies, cookies, teas, coffee, finger sandwiches, fancy breads, and jams.

Forest and Anna were very touched by all the trouble

their friends went through to make this an unforgettable evening.

Pastor blessed the food, and everyone ate.

After they were done eating, Holly talked to the women about wedding plans. Sara then talked to everyone about bringing Larry home. No one objected to Sara's request.

Anthony then shot a look to both Pastor Peter and Ruth.

"Shall we tell them?" Anthony asked Ruth.

"If you wish," Ruth said lovingly to Anthony.

"Pastor?" Anthony said.

"Yes, Anthony, please," Pastor said.

All in the room held their breath. You could cut the tension with a knife.

"Friends, you all know how important you are to us. You know we consider all of you like family. We love you all deeply. We did not do this to hurt you. Yesterday evening in a small quiet ceremony, Ruth and I gave lives to each other before God and Pastor," Anthony said with a hint of nervousness in his voice.

"Why didn't you tell us?" Sara said, almost bitterly.

"Sara, we love you. We got married quietly because we did not want to overshadow this day or the upcoming wedding," Anthony revealed, hoping Sara would understand. Sara turned away. Ruth walked over to Sara and took her hand.

"Sara, in this late stage of our lives, Anthony and I just wanted to dedicate our lives to each other. We Hope you understand," Ruth said, trying to ease Sara's pain.

"Of course, Aunt Ruth. I understand," Sara said, smiling. Then Sara kissed her aunt on the forehead and walked over and with a warm embrace welcomed Anthony to the family.

"This calls for a toast," Turner said.

"It sure does," Mr. Frederick said.

Helena then started pouring some ginger ale into everyone's glass. When she finished pouring the glasses, everyone raised them.

Turner then said, "To the happy couple, we wish you peace, we wish you joy, and we wish you all of God's blessings. To Forest and Anna, we wish you never-ending smiles, a house full of laughter, and love with your family."

"Here, here!" Ronnie cried out. The others followed. The night ended when Pastor Peter said, "Everyone, we must save some of our celebration of spirit for the weddings." Everyone went home.

Chapter 16

Dear Officer Danny, I am writing to request the body of Larry Frank, my husband. I want to bring him home and give him a proper burial in my family's plot. Please. Thank you. Your sister in Christ, Sara Wilson Frank.

Officer Danny was never unnerved by anything, but faith in Sara made him uneasy. How could he face a young woman that was so respected by her friends? If maybe he would have revealed the truth to her earlier, she would have been reunited with Larry before he passed on. His guilt ate away at his soul. If bringing Larry home would bring her the peace and closure she needed, he would grant her request.

. . .

Mr. Frederick said to Turner, "May I speak with you a moment alone?"

"Yes, of course," Turner said, hearing the urgency in his voice. "Are you okay? Is Helena okay?" Turner asked.

"Yes, find but I need to talk to you about Helena," Mr. Frederick replied. Turner looked at him with a puzzled face. "I don't know if I will be a good enough husband for Helena," Mr. Frederick said.

"Freddy, what you are experiencing is a case of cold

feet. Many brides and grooms go through this. Helena loves you, and you love her, and remember what the Bible says. Perfect love casts out fear," Turner said, placing his hand on Mr. Frederick's shoulder.

"Thank you, Turner, for always being there for me," Mr. Frederick said, giving Turner a bear hug.

Turner returned the hug and said, "That's what brothers are for."

· · ·

"Mama, Papa, I know I have not been able to talk to you for a little while," Sara said, kneeling at the grave of her parents. "I need to talk to you about Larry," Sara said prayerfully. She then spoke the words of her heart to her parents. She then placed a red rose on her mother's headstone and a yellow on her father's. In prayerful medication, she kneeled on the grass. A gust of summer wind brushed against her cheek. "Thank you for answering me," Sara said. "Oh, Holly, I did not see you there," Sara said.

"I did not want to disturb you during your prayer. It looked like you were saying something important," Holly responded.

"Are you ready to work on your routine?" Sara asked.

"Yes, yes, I can't wait till they see us dance," Holly answered. Holly and Sara worked on their dance steps for hours, and then they broke bread together.

· · ·

Officer Danny and Shady Woods' undertaker dug up the small wooden casket from Potter's Field. "I shall be back in a few days," he told the undertaker. The two men then loaded the casket on to a wagon and draped it with a black cloth.

• • •

"Nurse Lilly, are you ready to go?" asked Dr. Friendsmore.

"Yes," she replied. "We will go pick up Mr. Pepper and Dr. Olson, and then we will be on our way."

• • •

"Oh, Holly, baby, my sweet girl, you look beautiful!" her mother cried as Holly tried on her wedding dress for one last fitting.

The other women in the room gasped at the sight of her elegance.

"Helena, are you ready to try on yours?" Summer asked.

"I've have waited a lifetime and can't wait another moment," Helena replied. Kim and Sister Victoria helped Helena slip on her dress. Sara could not catch her breath when she saw her best friend in her wedding gown.

"You look like a princess!" Sara cried. Holly spun around in her dress.

"Sara, this will be beautiful to dance in," Holly proclaimed. Holly's dress was made of white satin. It had no rhinestones or pearls like Helena's dress had, but it had one unique feature: stitched by her mama's hands in the white satin were red heart-shapes; all in the satin you could see little hearts. All the women commented on how they never saw anything like that before.

Sister Victoria then tried on her dress. It was a seafoam green color. It was made of cotton. Ruth tried on her dress. It was baby blue, also made of cotton.

· · ·

The men were back on the Miller farm trying on their suits for the wedding. Mr. Frederick would be wearing a sky-blue suit. Little Ronnie would be wearing a gray suit. After the men tried on their suits, they looked over the ground where the wedding party would take place. They were all impressed.

Pastor Peter then announced that he must get back to the church. He still had to pick out the readings for the wedding. The wedding was to take place in three days, and there was still so much to do.

· · ·

Officer Danny passed a huge cotton field on the way to Summerville Heights. He thought about what he would say to Sara when he met her face-to-face. He knew he was drawing close to Summerville Heights, and there were butterflies in his stomach. When he got to Summerville Heights' county line, he paused and said a prayer.

Officer Danny could not bear to deliver the body to Sara's home. So he went to the church instead. There he found kind Pastor Peter. He told the pastor why he was there. Pastor talked with him for a while, and then he told Officer Danny to wait at the church while he gathered the townspeople for a service for Larry's soul.

One by one, house by house, Pastor delivered his news of the service. When Pastor got to Sara's house, he found that Turner was already there comforting her.

Sara was dressed in a black dress; on her head was a black kerchief.

"Sara, are you ready, dear?" Pastor said tenderly.

Turner took Sara's hand and held it tight. He looked deep into Sara's eyes, and said, "The Lord comforts those who mourn. He will not let their tears go unnoticed."

Sara, Turner, and Pastor returned to the church. When they arrived, everyone in town was there dressed in black. A young man approached Sara, saying, "I am very sorry for your loss, Miss Sara." His voice was filled with caring concern.

"How did you know Larry?" Sara asked.

"My name is Officer Danny." No more introductions were needed.

"Pastor, Turner, I need to talk to Officer Danny alone," Sara said. The men left her alone with the officer. Sara then turned to Officer Danny and said, "I want to know about Larry."

"Well, miss, what would you like to know?" Officer Danny asked.

"First tell me how he came to the law," Sara said.

"He came to me because he knew he did wrong by hitting you. He couldn't live with himself," Officer Danny said compassionately.

Sara then asked the officer all the questions that had been haunting her since the fire. Officer Danny did not want to tell Sara, but he said that Larry was burnt really bad and refused medical treatment because he knew that Sara was suffering too. He also told Sara he died from an infection.

Sara was shaken to the core. Officer Danny gave her comfort by telling her that because of Sara's love, Larry became a changed man. Officer Danny hid his emotions. He told her one last time how sorry he was and then left.

Turner was peeking out the doors of the church. He

saw Officer Danny leave. He then went to Sara. "Sara, are you okay?" he asked gently.

Sara's only response was, "He will give me beauty for my ashes."

Turner needed no more words. Turner took Sara by the hand, and together they walked into the church.

The service inside the church was a pitiful one. In front of the pulpit was the wooden casket that held Larry's body. Everyone was crying, but when Sara took her seat, they held back so they would not add to Sara's pain.

Pastor Peter, looking into Sara's eyes, read this Scripture: "Luke 2:25: 'Now there was a man in Jerusalem called Simon, who was righteous and devout. He was waiting for the consolation of Israel and the Holy Spirit was upon him. It had been revealed to him by the Holy Spirit that he would not die before he had seen the Lord's Christ. Moved by the Spirit, he went into the temple courts. When the parents brought in the Christ child to do for him what the custom of the Lord required, Simon took him in his arms and praised God saying: "Sovereign Lord, as you have promised, you now dismiss your servant in peace."'"

Before Pastor could say another word, Sara brushed away a tear and walked over to the casket.

"I love you. I forgive you. Go in peace. Goodbye, my dear Larry."

Moved by what they had seen Sara do, one by one, the townspeople walked over to Larry's casket and told him he was forgiven. Sara watched silently as she saw her friends forgive the only man she ever loved.

The men of the town loaded the casket on to the Miller wagon. Silently and sadly, horses, men, and women followed the wagon to Sara's family cemetery. They laid Larry to rest. And then Sara laid a white lily on top of his headstone. She said, "Your love for me was pure." Only Turner heard her whisper it. Sara then asked to be alone. All her friends respected her wishes and left. That night Sara only dreamed happy dreams about Larry.

• • •

It was the night before the wedding. Nurse Lilly, Mr. Pepper, Dr. Friendsmore, and Dr. Olson arrived in Summerville Heights. It was a crystal clear night. When they looked up at the sky, they could see the stars for miles and miles.

They went to Old Doc's office first to talk to him. When Old Doc explained that Sara had just buried Larry, they were very concerned for her.

"How is she holding up?" they asked.

Doc Benson replied, "Surprisingly well. Her faith is carrying her through."

They were very relieved to hear that. Old Doc showed them hospitality; he offered them food and drink. They ate. Then Old Doc said, "You must be tired from your trip. You can all use an exam room to nap in. Nurse Lilly, you can use my bedroom."

"Thank you," they all declared at once. Old Doc let them sleep for a solid few hours. It was early in the morning when they awoke.

• • •

The sun was bright and hot that morning. The air was still. The ground was dry, and the humidity ate away at the tree leaves. Holly sat at the edge of her bed.

"Dear Lord, help me to be a good wife, and if you will it, a good mother," she whispered.

Summer knocked on her daughter's bedroom door. "Miss Ruth is here to help you fix your hair," Summer said.

"Thank you, Mom. I will be out in a moment," Holly responded.

Adam could not believe that his baby girl was getting married today.

• • •

"Forest, should we dress Sara Faith in her lace pink dress or her white one?" Anna asked.

"The brides should only be wearing white today, dear," Forest answered kindly.

"You are right. I think I will dress both girls in their light green dresses, the ones that have the hats to match," Anna replied.

"Yes, dear, that would be perfect." Forest smiled.

"Mama, do I look handsome?" little John Michael said. He came out of his sisters' bedroom wearing his shoes on the wrong feet, his little suit jacket inside out, and his tie as a belt. Anna and Forest could not help but smile at their sweet young son.

"Very handsome, but can I just fix you up a bit?" Forest asked.

John Michael replied with a stubborn "no." Anna got the girls dressed; then she helped John Michael. John Michael looked at himself in his mirror.

"I get married too," he said cheerfully.

"Yes, someday," Anna replied.

Forest watched the children as Anna got dressed.

Anna wore her hair in tight curls that hugged her around her face. She wore a pale green dress that Summer had made for the occasion. Forest was speechless when he saw how beautiful she looked.

Forest wore a gray suit with a white shirt and his father's pin-striped tie. "Anna, you better get going. Don't you have to meet the girls at Summer's house?" Forest asked.

"Yes, I better leave," Anna and. Forest gave a quick peck to each other before Anna left.

• • •

Ruth arrived at Summer's house wearing her baby blue dress. It was floor length. It had pretty pearl buttons going up the neckline in the back of the dress. She wore a little blush she had borrowed from Amy Carrie.

"Good morning, Ruth," Summer said.

"Good morning, and where is the pretty bride to be?" Ruth asked.

"She will be out in a moment. Would you like a spot of tea?" Summer asked.

"No, thank you. I don't want to spill anything on this pretty dress," Ruth answered.

"Sweetheart, Sister Victoria is here," Adam called from the kitchen.

"Please send her back," Summer called from the other room. Sister was wearing her sea-foam green dress Summer made. She was wearing a pearl necklace around her thin neck. Light-green eye shadow made her eyes vibrant and bright. Her hair was pulled up in a bun; the bun was held up by a pretty white comb.

"Please excuse me for a moment. I want to check on Holly," Summer excused herself politely.

Ruth and Sister made small talk while they waited for Summer and Holly to come back.

When Holly came into the room, her face was beaming with happiness. Sister grabbed her hand and said, "You are going to make a beautiful bride."

• • •

After Sara ate her breakfast, she slipped on her beautiful peach-colored gown and glass slippers. *Now what am I going to do with my hair?* she thought to herself. Then she had an idea. She went outside to her garden and picked a white lily to wear in it. She let pretty curls embrace her face and stuck the lily behind her ear. She then painted her finger and toenails with pink polish. She put on lipstick, blush, and eye shadow. Helena gave her to wear. She was pleased by her own appearance.

Sara then headed over to Summer's and Adam's house. When she arrived, all the women in town were there, except for Helena and Amy Carrie.

• • •

On the Miller farm, the men were busy making last minute preparations of the grounds.

"Looks perfect," Adam said.

"Do we have enough chairs out?" Mr. Frederick worried.

"Yes," Ronnie answered. It was a perfect day for a wedding. The sun was shining in agreement, and there was a cool breeze coming off the Miller pond.

Little Ronnie was nervously pacing around the yard.

He was dressed in a fine-looking suit, his hair was slicked back, and he had a white rose pinned to his suit.

The other groom, Mr. Frederick, was wearing a fine-looking suit. He had silver cuff links on. His hair was parted, but it had a little wave to it. The other men were dressed in their best suits.

• • •

Pastor Peter was making last minute adjustments to the church. He was going over his sermon and readings. The church looked prettier than he had ever seen it before. On the small altar were flower arrangements Sara and Kim had made from their gardens. Sara made a lily arrangement with pink, white, and yellow lilies. Kim had made a rose arrangement with red, purple, and green roses. One sat on the left side of the altar, the other on the right. Pastor Peter's pulpit was draped with a white satin cloth. On the other side of the small wooden pews were white, laced bows. As the pastor took in the church's beauty, he was filled with great contentment.

• • •

"Nurse Lilly, I would like you to meet all my friends," Sara said happily.

Nurse Lilly was dressed in a yellow sundress. She was wearing a pretty wide-brim hat and pretty high-heel shoes. One by one, Sara introduced Lilly to her loving friends.

"Pleased to make your acquaintance, y'all," she said with a look of friendship.

"Well, I think it's about time to get both brides dressed," Kim happily announced. The women helped each one of the brides. Sara helped Helena put on her corset, slip, and shoes, and then slip over her wedding dress without messing Helena's hair. Next, the women helped Holly Amber.

When they were both dressed, the women's hearts were filled with love. Helena just looked like Cinderella. Her dress was a long, flowing gown; the pearl beadwork and lace hugged every curve of her body. She had her hair upswept with just a few curls hugging her cheek. In her hair was baby's breath. She wore light-pink lipstick and blush. She wore a pretty pair of clipped on pearl earrings. Around her neck was one strand of delicate pearls. On her left wrist a delicate pearl bracelet.

Holly's dress was a more simple dress with one exception: the heart stitch work. Her train was longer. In her ears she wore a pair of diamond earrings that Kim let her borrow. Her hair hung down in curls. She wore a pretty lace veil and a pair of her grandmother's dance slippers. She wore her nails long with pink nail polish and only a little bit of eye shadow.

Ruth looked around the room. She said, "If I may say so myself, we all look like beauty queens." The women all laughed.

Sara then handed both brides a very special gift: two beautiful bouquets of white lilies tied with pink ribbon. "Grown with love," Sara said, smiling.

Helena felt overwhelmed with wedding jitters and began to cry.

"Now don't do that. If you cry, we will all cry and ruin our makeup," Sara made a joke. With that, the women laughed again.

• • •

"The horses and buggies are ready," Doc Friendsmore said to the other men. Even the horses were dressed fancy for the occasion. Doc Friendsmore dressed his buggy with white bows. Liberty was wearing a pretty new saddle; a wreath made of white lilies hung around his neck. Freedom, that was ready to pull the other wagon, had a wreath of red flowers around his neck. Both wagons had blankets down inside them so no one would get dirty. One wagon was to carry the men to church; the other, the women.

Ronnie gathered up the men.

"Are you ready to get married?" Turner said happily to Mr. Frederick and Little Ronnie.

"Sure am," Mr. Frederick said.

"Yes, sir," Little Ronnie answered."

"Are you nervous?" Ronnie asked his son.

"Papa, you and Mama were true examples of how a marriage should be, so I am not nervous at all." With that, Little Ronnie hugged his father tenderly.

As the men loaded into the buggy, both grooms thanked the men for making their dreams come true. The townspeople also planned another surprise for both brides and grooms. The two grooms saw the surprise first as the buggy took them down Happiness Trail. Happiness Trail was covered with pink rose petals and white paper streamers. Mr. Frederick and Little Ronnie also saw a sign that Forest had made. It read, "Congratulations! May Happiness Trail be the path leading to all your dreams." Both grooms were very touched.

When they arrived at the church, Pastor Peter greeted them all with a smile. Mr. Pepper also had a very special surprise for them. He knew how to play the piano, so he would be providing the music. Pastor showed all the men where to stand. Some of the men would be walking down the aisle; the ones who were not took their seats.

Anthony went to go pick up the woman.

"All you ladies look so beautiful," Anthony said. When he looked at his wife, Ruth, he had tears in his eyes because she looked radiant. Holly and Helena were speechless when they saw how pretty the wagon and horses looked. Anthony helped the two brides into the wagon first and then the rest of the women.

For a moment, Sara felt a touch of jealousy because she wished she would have had a wedding day like this. Her jealousy quickly faded when she saw how happy Helena was.

The two brides cried when they saw how their friends decorated Happiness Trail.

Chapter 17

When they arrived at the little white church, they could hear the birds in the trees singing a love song for them. Anthony and all the women got out of the wagon. Pastor Peter met everyone at the doors of the church.

"Like two angels that fell from heaven," Pastor said of the pretty brides. He then threw a compliment to all the rest of the ladies.

Pastor then lined everyone up on how they were supposed to walk in. "Does anyone have any questions?" Pastor asked. They all responded with a unified no. "I will tell Mr. Pepper to start the music then," Pastor said. With a wave of Pastor's hand, Mr. Pepper played "Ave Maria" on the beautiful pipe organ. The music echoed through Summerville Heights, and it might have even been heard in nearby towns. Pastor slowly walked down the aisle with Amy Carrie. When he reached the pulpit, Amy took her seat. Doc Friendsmore, Dr. Olson, and Nurse Lilly sat behind her.

The next couple to walk down the aisle was Ruth and Anthony. Ruth was wearing the brightest smile anyone had ever seen on her face. Following Ruth and Anthony was Ronnie, who escorted Kim and Sister Victoria. Sister Victoria tried in a desperate attempt to hold back tears as she was walking down the aisle but failed. Mr. Pepper now switched to playing, "This Little Light of Mine." Summer and Adam were the next to go down the aisle. Summer held on tightly to Adam's arms because he was her anchor. When everyone saw the next couple, tears came flowing from their eyes. It was Turner and Sara. Sara wanted to dance down the aisle; she could hardly contain her happiness. Nurse Lilly felt like the breath was sucked out of her when she saw how beautiful Sara looked. Dr. Friendsmore started clapping, and Dr. Olson's face was full or pride and joy.

Mr. Pepper then started to play the "Wedding March." Everyone in the church rose to his or her feet. All heads turned to the church doors. The doors opened, and the two brides stepped in. Holly and Helena walked down the aisle arm in arm.

Mr. Frederick's heart pounded so hard he thought he was going to pass out. Little Ronnie stayed calm, but he was so excited. Mr. Frederick reached out and took Helena's hand. Little Ronnie reached out and took Holly's hand. All the other guests took their seats.

Helena, Mr. Frederick, Holly, and Little Ronnie now turned and faced Pastor Peter. Pastor Peter looked at the two lovely couples and smiled.

He then turned to all his other guests and said, "Welcome, friends, on this happy, glorious occasion. God gave us love in his Son, Jesus Christ. We gather together today to celebrate the beautiful love between a man and a woman. "Love is patient, love is kind. It does not envy, it does not boast, it is not proud. It is not rude … It always protects, always trusts, always Hopes, always preserves. Love never fails." Holly began crying. Little Ronnie tenderly wiped away a tear from her eye with his handkerchief. Pastor went on, "We are here as witness of the heavenly bond God has formed between these four beautiful people."

Sara looked around the church and saw the happiness encircling everyone there. From the corner of her eye, she saw Kim and Ronnie holding hands. Summer had her head on Adam's shoulder. Ruth and Anthony were in a warm embrace. She also noticed how sweet Turner looked.

Pastor Peter said, "I will now ask Helena and Mr. Frederick to state their intentions."

"Pastor, we have written our own wedding promises," Mr. Frederick stated.

Pastor replied, "You may read them now if you wish."

Mr. Frederick read his first. He looked deep into Helena's soulful eyes and said, "Helena, I can't promise you days without rain, but I can promise you I will always love you. I can't promise you wealth, but I can promise you if the stars fall from the heavens, I will give you the moon. I can't promise you a day without sickness, but I do promise you the offer of my gentle touch. I promise you today, before God, that I will love you until the day he calls me home." With those beautiful words, many emotions stirred in everyone's hearts.

Helena took a deep breath. She took Mr. Frederick's hand and said, "When I was a young girl, I used to pray for an angel to be sent down from heaven. I never knew his name until I met you. Frederick, I promise you today, as angels as our witnesses, that I will sacrifice my last breath if I knew it would make one of your dreams come true. I love you, Freddy."

Sara began sobbing. Turner put his arm around Sara and whispered, "It's okay." He knew Sara was thinking about Larry.

Summer also could not hold back the tears and began sobbing. Adam wrapped his arms her and held her in a tight embrace. Pastor then said, "That was beautiful."

He then turned to Holly and Little Ronnie. "Have you prepared anything?"

"Yes," Little Ronnie replied. Little Ronnie placed his hand over Holly's heart and said a scripture from Proverbs. He read, "A wife of noble character, who can find her? She is far more worth the rubies. Her husband has full confidence in her and lacks nothing of value. She is clothed with strength and dignity. She can laugh at the days to come. She speaks with wonder, and faithful instruction is on her tongue. Many women do noble things, but you surpass them all."

Holly then responded with scripture from Song of Songs. Everyone was moved. Pastor then read from John. "God is love. Whoever lives in love lives in God and God in him." Pastor then said, "Do you have the rings?" Forest then brought little John Michael, who was the ring bearer, up to the altar. Pastor blessed the rings. Little Ronnie slipped on a gold band with the inscription "Forever my love" on Holly's finger. Mr. Frederick slipped on a simple silver band on Helena's finger. Pastor then said, "What God has joined, man must not divide." Laughing, Pastor then said, "You may kiss your brides."

Little Ronnie gently brushed Holly's lips, while Mr. Frederick gave Helena a long, drawn-out, movie kiss. Everyone in the church cheered and let out a big round of applause.

Mr. Pepper then started to play "Oh Promise Me." Nurse Lilly got caught up in the moment and began to sing. She had an angelic voice. Sara then began to sing with her. It turned out to be a beautiful moment in the ceremony.

Pastor Peter stood by the door, along with all the other guests, congratulating the newly married couples.

"It was a beautiful, moving ceremony," Turner said.

"Yes, heaven inspired," Helena agreed.

The men loaded into one wagon and the woman in the other. There were still many surprises to come on this special day. As the two wagons filled with happy friends rode down Happiness Trail, Helena began to sing "Oh Happy Day." Everyone joined in. Suddenly the valley was filled with their sweet voices. Even the wild animals seemed to enjoy this singing. A deer and a baby fawn appeared out of nowhere and stopped and listened.

When they arrived back at the Miller farm, Holly and Helena were overwhelmed by the sight of it. It was decorated from top to bottom. On all the pretty trees, white bells hung from the branches. In the pond were pretty floating candles of red, pink, and yellow colors. There were colorful balloons and a beautiful arch covered with climbing roses. There was also a white tent; underneath the tent were six white tables and chairs to match. The tables were covered with lace tablecloths. Sitting on top of the tables were vases with roses in them and a single white candle in a silver candleholder.

"It's breathtaking," Helena boasted.

"Only the best for my bride," Mr. Frederick said.

Holly ran to Little Ronnie with pure excitement in her voice. "It's all I could have ever dreamed and more."

"I'm glad, sweetheart," Little Ronnie replied

"Hello, I am Mr. Taylor," a tall lean man said.

Just then Dr. Friendsmore and Dr. Olson said, "Mr.

Taylor is a photographer. He is our wedding gift to the brides and grooms."

"A photographer?" Helena said.

"Oh, thank you, thank you, thank you!" Holly grabbed them both and gave them a hug.

"How can we repay you for your kindness?" Mr. Frederick asked.

"Just be happy," Dr. Olson said.

"Where shall I set up?" Mr. Taylor asked.

"Over by the pond," Ronnie directed. When Mr. Taylor finished setting up by the pond, he took pictures. First he took pictures of the brides, then their grooms. He then took pictures of the brides and grooms together and the guests. By the time he was done taking all the pictures, he used three rolls of film. After the photographer was done taking all the pictures, Anna sang a beautiful love song. Mr. Frederick and Helena danced. Then Mr. Pepper sang a song, and Holly and Little Ronnie danced.

All the guests were getting hungry, so Kim announced that it was time to eat. Pastor said a heartfelt prayer. Turner added to the prayer from Galatians 5:22. "But the fruit of the spirit is love, joy, peace, patience, kindness, goodness, faithfulness, gentleness, and self control."

"Before everyone eats, I would like to make a toast," Adam announced. "May God's love always be in your heart, in your mind, and on your lips. May his peace always fill your home. Congratulations to my daughter and son," Adam said joyfully.

"I too would like to make a toast," Turner said. "May the love in your hearts that you feel today only grow stronger with time."

"Well, since everyone else is making a toast, I would

like to say something too," said Ronnie. "Mr. Frederick, you have been like a brother to me. I would just like to say I wish you and Helena a lifetime of happiness. To my sweet boy, Little Ronnie, and his new wife, Holly, I would like to say you have given me great joy, and I Hope the Lord will bless you tenfold with the joy you have given me." With that, everyone raised their glasses and toasted the newly married couples.

On the huge white table there were king size dishes. Kim, Ruth, and Sister had been cooking for three days straight. There was pot roast, ham, meat loaf, potatoes, gravy, carrots, peas, yams, collard greens, corn, and turnips. There were also mouth-watering desserts: homemade apple pie, pudding, ice cream, watermelon, strawberry short cake, and cookies. Old Doc said in a laughing tone, "Well, if the whole United States Army comes to Summerville Heights tonight, we would certainly have enough food to feed them."

"I agree," Amy said, laughing. Everyone enjoyed the food so much. No one could turn down a second plate. They sat and talked about how beautiful the wedding was.

Dusk fell on Summerville Heights. Ronnie and Forest lit all the candles. It was a romantic setting. Love hung heavy in the air.

Turner saw Sara whisper something in Mr. Pepper's ear. Then Holly and Sara abruptly got up from their chairs they were sitting in. Mr. Pepper then said, "Ladies and gentlemen, we have a request from bride Holly for everyone to remain seated." Everyone looked at them with wonderment and excitement in their eyes.

Chapter 18

Mr. Pepper walked over to the Miller piano that was taken outside for the special occasion. He began to play a beautiful melody. Nurse Lilly recognized the melody as the wedding waltz. She began to sing to the harmony of the piano. Suddenly, Holly appeared and began to dance. Sara soon joined her. Like one graceful instrument, the movement of their bodies became one with the music. Freely, gracefully, and tenderly, Sara's heart became in sync with the music. She closed her eyes and got lost in the haunting melody that was now like her own heartbeat.

Everyone watched in amazement as the two women danced like birds in flight. With each step, it was like they were walking on a cloud. Sara leaped and moved like an angel with wings. Everyone was in tears. Helena looked at her friend Sara and remembered how she used to dance.

"Bravo!" Forest called out.

Old Doc called out, "I will be next in line to dance with you, Sara!"

Dr. Friendsmore said, "Sara promised me first." When the women were done dancing, everyone told them how graceful they were. Turner could not find the words to express how touched he was watching them dance, so he quickly got two roses and gave each of them one.

"The celebration has really begun now," Pastor said. Sara danced with Old Doc next. By the end of the night, everyone was dancing. Turner was the last one to dance with Sara.

"What a perfect ending to a perfect night," Sara whispered.

Mr. Frederick overheard what Sara said. He then turned to Sara. "Not over yet, my dear." Sara smiled at him.

"What was that?" Ruth asked, looking up in the sky. *Bang, bang, pop, pop,* they heard. Everyone's eyes were turned toward the sky now.

"Fireworks," Mr. Frederick said. It was Anthony's gift to this special night. Everyone sat in chairs and watched the colorful bursts. Red, green, purple, orange, and yellow lit up the midnight sky.

"What can we say to all of you except that we love you," Helena said sadly because she knew the night was almost over.

"Who is that?" Old Doc said. All eyes now turned to a man coming from the dark down Happiness Trail. No one knew who this man was. The man rode a black horse. He was wearing a big black cowboy hat and a pair of snakeskin boots. He was wearing a fine suit. In his hand, he held a leather bag. As the man got closer to the crowd, everyone saw he was a good-looking man in his twenties.

"Sorry, folks. I do not mean to disturb your celebration. My name is Davis Kindfellow."

Ronnie stepped forward. "Who do you have business with here?" he asked in a ticked off voice.

"A Mrs. Sara Wilson Frank," the man said.

"What do you want with Sara?" Turner asked in a protective big-brother voice.

"Well, it's a matter of personal business," the man said.

"I am Sara. Whatever you need to say to me, you can say in front of my family," Sara said in a no-nonsense manner.

"I am a lawyer. It has taken me a long time to find you. I come from a town in South Carolina called Teardrops Falls. I don't know quite how to explain this."

"What do you want with me? I've never been to Teardrops Falls," Sara stated.

"Miss Sara, I was the lawyer for your late husband. After the fire, Mr. Larry lived in Teardrops Falls, and that's how our paths crossed." Mr. Kindfellow said.

"But Larry turned himself in." Ruth looked confused.

"Yes, he did, but not before he found out where his mother was. Your late sister was living there. He went there to see if she could help him."

"My late sister?" Ruth started to cry.

"Yes, I am sorry. She passed away right after Larry turned himself in," Mr. Kindfellow explained.

"But what does all of this have to do with me?" Sara asked.

"Larry reunited with his mother, but Larry and his mother knew they were sick and would not survive long," The man went on.

Pastor then interrupted. "This family has gone through enough heartache. Are you here to bring more?" Pastor said with fury in his voice.

"No, sir. I am very sorry to be the bearer of this news, but I promised that I would find Sara. Larry and his mother left you some money to open your own dance studio because Larry knew that was your dream," Mr. Kindfellow explained.

"What? I can't believe it!" Sara said with a strange look. Everyone stood in disbelief.

"But where did Larry get that kind of money?" Ruth asked.

Mr. Kindfellow then explained. "When your sister left her family, she went on to marry a man with money. When he passed, she got everything."

"I can't accept this money!" Sara screamed.

"Sara, you are entitled to it. Maybe this is Larry's way of making up for what he did," Sister softly beckoned.

"Maybe, but how would I ever run my own dance studio? I know nothing about business. I am just a small-town girl," Sara said.

"Well, that's where your aunt and I come in. We will take care of the business aspect; you concentrate on the dance part," Anthony said.

"My own dance studio," Sara said with a dreamy look in her eyes.

"I will certainly be your first client," Holly said happily.

"Sara, this check is for $2, 000," Mr. Kindfellow said.

"Wow! I can't believe it!" Sara said.

Mr. Kindfellow handed Sara the check.

"Can we get you a plate?" Sister asked the man.

"I thank you, but I must be heading back," he replied.

"Well then, we will fix you some food to take on your journey," Helena suggested. Sister Victoria handed the man the plate.

"Thank you kindly," he said, tipping his hat toward Sister. He got on his big black horse and left.

As everyone watched him ride out of sight, they were filled with questions. Sara stared at the money in her hands. Turner then said, "Sara, think of it as Larry's last gift to you,"

"I still can't believe that he and his mom did this for me," Sara said.

"Yes, after all this time, you will have your own dance studio," Ruth said.

It was getting late into the night; everyone was tired. So everyone congratulated the brides and grooms with one last kiss and headed back to their homes. Sister Victoria said good night first. Ruth and Anthony walked Sara back home. On their walk down Happiness Trail, they discussed about Larry, his gift to Sara, and what the future would hold.

Little Ronnie and Holly went back to their new two-bedroom apartment that was built on the back of the Miller farmhouse.

Helena and Mr. Frederick now to had a small house. It was near the dirt road leading to the pasture. Ronnie had taken some money out of his savings to build a new addition.

"I can't believe we have our own home," Mr. Frederick said to his lovely bride.

"I can't believe it either," Helena said.

Night fell upon sleepy little Summerville Heights. The stars kissed the midnight sky. The moon sprinkled its glow across the dream of Summerville Heights' residents. Everyone's eyes shut to a deep star-lit sleep.

Chapter 19

The next morning Sara awoke refreshed and happy. She made her breakfast and then went outside. She knelt beside Larry's grave. "Oh, Larry, if we had more time together, I wish I could have read your heart while you were still here. Thank you, Larry, for your gift. Why couldn't you come back after the fire, Larry. No matter what, I still love you so much," Sara whispered. Then she looked at her mother's and father's graves. She sobbed. "Mama, you taught me all I know about dancing. How can I open a dance studio without you?" Then a butterfly landed on her hand. *Whenever you get scared, just remember to count the butterflies.* The words echoed in Sara's heart, and then she was no longer scared.

. . .

"Good morning, Mrs. Miller," Little Ronnie said, beaming to Holly.

"Good morning, Mr. Miller," Holly said with a glow of a new bride. "I can't believe I am waking up next to you," Holly said with a look of love in her eyes. Ronnie responded by giving Holly a kiss.

• • •

"Helena, my darling wife, you don't have to fix me breakfast in bed," Mr. Frederick said, blushing.

"You better get used to being pampered," Helena responded.

• • •

Amy awoke early that morning too. She wanted to get to the Miller farm to help clean up from the wedding reception. When she arrived, Kim, Holly, and Helena were already cleaning. The men went out to do their chores. Turner was out milking a cow when he saw Amy. He greeted her and directed her to where the other women were.

• • •

Sister went into town to talk to Ruth and Anthony. She was very concerned about Sara. She thought the recent events that Sara had been through were just too much for one person.

"I do not know if it's a good idea for Sara to take this money and open a dance studio," Sister voiced her objection.

"Sister, with all due respect, it is Sara's decision. Sara is one tough lady who can handle herself," Ruth replied.

"What do you think, Anthony?" Sister asked.

"I think with all of our support and help this will be good for Sara," he replied.

"Maybe I am just old fashioned, but I am worried," Sister said again.

"Why doesn't anyone ask Sara what Sara thinks?"

They were all stunned when they heard Sara speak those words.

"Sara, I do not mean to imply that you can't pull it off," Sister said.

"Sister, you are like a grandma to me. I love you for worrying about me, but I can handle this, and I want to do this," Sara said wholeheartedly.

"Sara, of course I will help you anyway I can." Sister gave Sara a hug.

"Well, there is one thing you can do for me right now. I want to have a meeting at church tonight. Could you let everyone know?" Sara eyes pleaded.

"Of course. I am on my way to see Old Doc now," Sister said.

"I am too." Sara said goodbye and headed to Old Doc's office.

It was a beautiful summer's day. Sara enjoyed the smell of jasmine and peach trees. "Good day, my friends," Sara said.

"God day," Old Doc responded. "I am glad you are here. Nurse Lilly, Dr. Friendsmore, Dr. Olson, and I have some exciting news to share with you," Old Doc said, smiling.

"News?" Sara asked.

"Yes. Sara you better sit down," Doc Friendsmore said.

"Old friends, I don't know if I can take any more," Sara said nervously.

"No, no, let me put your mind at ease; this is terrific news." Doc smiled widely.

"Well, in that case, please have your lips spill it," Sara said with curiosity in her voice.

Old Doc said in a tender voice, "Sara, Lilly, Doc

Olson, Dr. Friendsmore, and I have decided to open up a practice here in Summerville Heights. With our community growing, I can't handle all the patients by myself. Dr. Friendsmore and Dr. Olson have advanced medicine that could help us, and Nurse Lilly has the healing touch people look for."

"Oh, that is so wonderful, and I support you 100 percent. You can work miracles and magic. Look what you did for me? You have been gifted by God to be healing angels on his earth," Sara said. She then embraced her friends. She then told them about the meeting at church.

"A meeting?" Old Doc asked.

"Yes, about the dance studio," Sara replied.

"Yes, we were hoping you would," Nurse Lilly said.

"You are not having reservations about me opening one, are you?" Sara asked, concerned.

"No, not at all," Old Doc said.

• • •

Forest was extremely excited when he came home from the mill. He came running into the house out of breath with his heart racing. He found Anna preparing food for the children. "Honey! Honey!" he called out.

"In the kitchen!" Anna called back.

"You won't believe it. I was at the mill. Turner was there, and…and…"

"Slow down, take a breath, sit down, and I will pour you some coffee," Anna said. Forest took a sip of his coffee and regained his composure. "Let me start over, honey. When I got to the mill, Turner was there talking to Mr. Pearlman. Mr. Pearlman agreed to donate all the lumber for Sara's studio. Also, he said he would sell Sara that beautiful piece of land by the creek for a $1,000."

"Really? You are not kidding?" Anna asked.

"No, sweetheart. Turner, the miracle worker, said something to him that really spoke to his heart," Forest said. Anna then told Forest about the church meeting.

• • •

Pastor was setting up some chairs in the fellowship hall. When the townspeople started to arrive, Sister was first to arrive as usual. Summer and Adam came next, then Old Doc, followed by Ruth and Anthony. Everyone came with anticipation in his or her hearts.

"Where is Sara?" Turner asked.

"She will be here soon. She wanted to give Morning Dew a wash down before she came," Old Doc answered.

Mr. Pearlman even came into town for this important meeting. Mr. Pearlman was an older man in his seventies. He was a widower, twice over. He had no children. When he was younger, he and his first wife invested their savings into the mill. He bought a piece of land three acres in Summerville Heights in Hopes of building a mill there. After his first and second wife passed, the land remained unused.

Sara came in to the meeting with a cool, confident look. "Good evening, my friends," Sara said.

"Hello," her friends responded.

Pastor then said, "Could everyone please take their seats."

Everyone did except Sara and Old Doc. Old Doc said to Sara, "You tell them your news first." Sara then told them about Mr. Pearlman and his generous offer. Mr.

Pearlman had gone to Sara's earlier in the day to make the offer. Sara was thrilled when she heard it; she accepted his offer without even thinking about it. Everyone in town was very excited too.

Sister Victoria was still very worried about Sara. She did not let her worry overshadow Sara's joy that night.

"Miss Summer, I would like you to make all the dance slippers and costumes," Sara explained. Summer was overjoyed. Sara went on to say, "Since I only have to pay Mr. Pearlman $1,000 for the land, I would like to give Pastor the rest of the money to be used however he sees fit in helping our town." Sara went on.

Everyone was very touched. "Sara, you keep the money. We appreciate your generosity, but we can not take something that belongs to you," her friends objected.

"I insist, after all you have done for me," Sara responded.

"Well, if it makes you happy," Pastor said. "But we will all decide what the money is to be used for," he went on to say.

"Agreed," Sara said.

Old Doc then got up and told everyone his news. The town was very happy. Then Sara had a great idea. "We can use some of the money to help extend the medical clinic!" Sara said happily.

"That's a great idea," everyone agreed.

Mr. Pearlman was very interested in Summerville Heights because he was planning to relocate there. Everyone was surprised by Mr. Pearlman's interest. Mr. Pearlman then explained his interest to the town folk. "I am tired of big city life. I want to spend my last days in Summerville Heights where I can have peace, quiet, kinship, and nature," he said.

"A new resident to Summerville Heights. We welcome you with open arms," Little Ronnie said.

"Mr. Pearlman, if you are looking for a place to live, my apartment behind the ice cream parlor has been standing empty ever since Anthony and I got married. If you would like to rent it, it's yours," Ruth said.

"Would it be okay if I look at it first?" Mr. Pearlman asked.

"I can show it to you right now if you like," Anthony answered.

"Yes, that would be perfect. Sara, I will tie up any loose ends about the land tomorrow," Mr. Pearlman stated.

"Sounds good," Sara responded,

Anthony, Ruth, and Mr. Pearlman went to look at the apartment. Sister Victoria spoke to Pastor and Amy about her reservations about Sara. Pastor Peter eased her fears. Sara then spoke to Turner privately about her dance studio. Everyone else went home.

Sara slept in a peaceful slumber that hot August night. Turner stayed awake praying for his friends,

"Oh, my God! Was that real, or was that a dream?" Sara quickly arose from her bed. Sara ran outside with her nightclothes on to Larry's grave. "Larry, I would have sworn you were just in the bedroom caressing my face, but I guess it was just wishful thinking. It was a good dream though, Larry," Sara softly whispered.

• • •

Turner was working on the farm with the other men when Old Doc came to visit. Doc wanted to ask them advice about the new practice. Kim set a place at the breakfast table for Old Doc, as well as everyone else in her growing family.

Sister Victoria spent the early morning hours reading her Bible and praying. Even though everyone in town was happy with the changes taking place, Sister could not shake her gut feeling that a terrible fate was about to fall on someone she loved.

Sara met with Mr. Pearlman, Ruth, and Anthony to work out the last minute details of the land sale. Mr. Pearlman was also going to rent Ruth's old apartment, so they worked out the details on that too.

"I will be back September 1 with my men to help build the studio," Mr. Pearlman said.

"Sounds good. It will give Ruth a chance to clean out the apartment too," Anthony said.

"I will see you all in September again," Mr. Pearlman said. After Mr. Pearlman departed from the land site, Sara, Ruth, and Anthony walked around on the land for a while. They discussed plans for the studio. They had lost track of time when they noticed it was near lunch hour.

On the other side of town Old Doc, Dr. Friendsmore, Dr. Olson, and Nurse Lilly were sitting around Doc's kitchen table discussing plans for the new clinic.

"Doc Olson, I do believe we can help a lot of people here by opening a free clinic," Old Doc said.

Doc Benson then said, "Yes, I do believe with your wisdom, my drive, Doc Olson's talent, and Nurse Lilly's tender, loving care, we will do a lot of good here."

Doc Friendsmore commented, "After lunch, I will show you the piece of land I have owned secretly for many years hoping that one day I would be able to build a more state-of-the-art medical clinic." Old Doc smiled.

"We are very anxious to see it," Nurse Lilly said.

"I have a very good feeling about this," Old Doc added.

Chapter 20

Holly was sewing some dresses when Anna arrived at the farm. Little John Michael went right away to Liberty and Freedom to pet them. They were both gentle horses, so Anna had no fear that they would hurt baby John. Sara Faith and Amanda Grace were dressed in little yellow dresses with ruffles.

"They look adorable," Holly commented.

"The girls are getting more active every day," Anna revealed.

"Look how nicely their hair is coming in," Kim said from the other room.

"Yes, I can't wait till they get a little older, as well as John Michael. It will be nice when I can start teaching younglings again," Anna said with a smile.

"When can we expect you and Little Ronnie to have a baby?" Kim asked.

"Mom, I just have to help Sara with her dance studio first," Holly said respectfully.

Turner, Little Ronnie, Ronnie, and Mr. Frederick had just gotten back from the general store. They filled the ladies in on how Mr. Pearlman handed the land over to Sara and that he would be back September 1 to start building the studio.

"That's wonderful," Kim said.

"I can't wait!" Holly Amber said with a voice filled with Hopeful dreams.

• • •

Amy and Sister Victoria were busy making plans to start back up the ladies Bible study group. They had stopped it after Sara's tragedy.

"It will sure be nice to sit over tea with our lady friends and study Scripture again," Amy said.

"It will also be nice to see some fresh new faces as well," Sister replied.

• • •

"Papa, I was thinking that it would be nice to give that little puppy we found to John Michael since we have not found the owner by now," Little Ronnie said.

"Well, if it okay with Forest and Anna, it's fine with me," Ronnie responded.

Sara met with Summer to go over possible dance slippers and dress designs for her new students. Summer thought of some great possibilities. Summer showed Sara some sketches she had been working on. Sara decided she liked the pink tutus with the white slippers the best.

• • •

The mill was abuzz with the news that Mr. Pearlman was retiring and moving to Summerville Heights. All the rough and tough men at the mill were very touched by the news that they would be helping make Sara's dreams come true.

Mr. Pearlman sat at his big metal desk overlooking the main work area of the mill. He tapped his fingers on a large stack of paper work; it was a bittersweet day for him. Today would be his last day working at the job he loved all his life. He knew in his heart the man that he had chosen to replace him and run the mill would do a fine job.

"Miss Linda, please send Forest in to my office," Mr. Pearlman asked his secretary. He had grown quite close to her over the years. She was a woman in her fifties; she had no former education but was as smart as a whip.

"Yes, sir," Miss Linda responded.

Forest came to Mr. Pearlman's office covered in sawdust from a hard day's work on his job. "Come in, come in; please sit down," Mr. Pearlman said, giving Forest a hardy handshake.

"Mr. Pearlman, have I done something wrong?" Forest asked nervously.

"No, quite the opposite, son. You are my loyal employee. You have given me years of dedicated service. You have never complained about anything." Mr. Pearlman smiled.

"I like my job very much. The men I work with are like blood brothers to my spirit," Forest answered.

"I am glad you do, son. That's why I have chosen you as my replacement," Mr. Pearlman said.

"Me? But I don't know how to run this yard," Forest said, lacking self-confidence.

"You know plenty; besides, what you don't know, Miss Linda will be here to help you with. Now why don't you take the rest of the day off to go celebrate with your family," Mr. Pearlman said, smiling.

"I won't let you down, sir," Forest said, gripping Mr. Pearlman's hand in a friendly handshake.

"I will see you on September 1, and we shall go over all the details then. Until then, I want you to have a vacation with your family until you take over the business," Mr. Pearlman said with a genuine smile.

"Yes, sir, I will," Forest replied. Forest raced home to tell Anna the great news. Together they dropped to their knees and gave their heavenly Father praises and thanks.

• • •

Summer was busy working on the dance slippers and tutus Sara ordered. She spent most of her days doing that.

Old Doc Benson, Nurse Lilly, Dr. Friendsmore, Dr. Olson, and Mr. Pepper spent most of their days drawing up plans for the new clinic.

Helena and Mr. Frederick worked on the little house when Mr. Frederick was not working the farm.

Holly and Little Ronnie also worked on their home, adding furniture piece-by-piece and decorating and painting.

Ruth and Anthony cleaned out the apartment for Mr. Pearlman.

It was a cooler summer day when Mr. Pearlman and his crew arrived in Summerville Heights to start work on Sara's studio. Everyone in town turned out for the ground-breaking ceremony. When the first plow was brought in, everyone cheered. Pastor Peter offered this prayer as the plow lifted its first pile of dirt: "Psalms 127:1: 'Unless the LORD builds the house, its builders labor in vain.' Psalms 128:1–2: 'Blessed are those who fear the Lord, who walk in his ways. You will eat the fruit of your labor; blessing and prosperity will be yours.'"

The excitement of the day drained the peaceful night. No one could sleep. Doc Benson decided to take a ride to check on his land and the frame of Summerville Heights's free clinic. The land was breathtaking. It was close to a babbling brook, red oak trees, and nature. It was the perfect place for people to find an escape from their illnesses. Doc Benson, being the kind God-fearing man he was, imagined all the children and sick moms and dads his healing hands would reach. "Thank you, Lord Jesus, for calling me into a profession that I could help so many others," Doc whispered.

• • •

Turner also sat awake that night praying. "Dear Lord, please give Sara the strength she needs to face the road she is traveling ahead." Turner eyes suddenly felt heavy, and he fell into a peaceful slumber.

• • •

Holly and Little Ronnie also lay awake that night. "Dear, I want to start a family," Little Ronnie said.

"I want to start a family too, Ronnie, but I would like to wait until Sara's studio is finished," Holly responded.

"But what if it takes a year or two or three. I know you love Sara. We all do, but must we put our dreams on hold?" Little Ronnie asked. They debated the issue throughout the night. When the morning sun arrived, they agreed to wait six months, and no matter what the progress was on the dance studio, they would try to start their family then.

• • •

"What's all this, sweetheart?" Forest asked with a gleam in his eye.

"It is your first day running the mill, so you will need all the energy you can get," Anna replied.

"Well, I will certainly have enough energy with all this food," Forest laughed with a smile. Anna had made hot oatmeal, pancakes, homemade maple syrup, coffee, bacon, and biscuits. Forest enjoyed the taste of the food on his tongue. He always drank his coffee black with sugar.

John drew his father a picture of him standing in front of the mill. John proudly gave it to his father.

"Daddy is the boss. Daddy is the boss," Little John sang throughout the kitchen.

"Thank you, baby John," Forest said as he took his last sip of his coffee. He then kissed his wife and children goodbye and headed toward the mill.

• • •

Summer spent the entire morning with Holly making dance slippers and tutus. Adam focused his effort on what he could do to help Old Doc with the medical clinic.

Mr. Frederick, Ronnie, and Turner rode to the next town to get the word out about the new dance studio and the new clinic.

Pastor and Amy went to Paradise Gates to help Mr. Pepper pack his and Dr. Olson's belongings.

Nurse Lilly and Doc Friendsmore stayed behind to help Old Doc with the building process.

Ruth, Anthony, and Sara met with Helena in the

afternoon to discuss how the grand opening of the dance studio should be planned.

Sister Victoria helped with all the preparations with the dance studio and the new clinic. Although sister was very happy that Sara's dreams were coming true, she still couldn't shake the horrible feeling in the pit of her stomach.

Mr. Pearlman quickly settled into his new life in Summerville Heights.

Chapter 21

Late summer turned into early fall. There was a slight chill in the air. The leaves were starting to change colors. The residents were busy working on the dance studio and the clinic.

Forest spent long days working at the mill. He was in charge of fifty men now. He was doing everything in his power not to let Mr. Pearlman down. On his lunch breaks, Forest would spend his time dreaming about Anna and the children. He spent most of his weeknights at the mill. He knew that someday all the long hours he was putting in would pay off for him and his family. In spite of all the late night suppers, Anna was a patient and supportive wife. Little Amanda and Sara Faith were now starting to cut teeth.

Anna spent a lot of her time getting ready to reopen Summerville Heights's schoolhouse. The schoolhouse was a small red brick building that sat at the end of Happiness Trail. Anna knew she would be having some new students soon with the opening of the dance school and the new clinic.

Sara, Ruth, and Anthony had spent the whole summer preparing for the grand opening of the dance school. They were all very anxious to see the fruit of their labor succeed.

Holly kept her promise to Little Ronnie, and they were now expecting their first child.

Mr. Frederick, Turner, and Ronnie had returned from neighboring towns with ten new students for Sara to teach dance to.

Doc Olson, Pastor Peter, Mr. Pepper, and Amy had returned to Summerville Heights too.

Helena, Sister, and Kim had spent the summer helping Anna with her children and getting the schoolhouse ready to open.

Summer, Holly, and Sara completed all the dance slippers and tutus.

Adam had also announced that he would be expanding his business as well.

Old Doc was pleased with the progress the builders had made with the new clinic.

Bobby Landers had also come to Summerville Heights that summer with a proposal to turn Old Doc's old office into a small hotel, which the townspeople agreed to.

Mr. Pearlman put his big heart into action and donated medical supplies for the opening of the new clinic. He also donated to Sara's dance school.

It was a cool brisk wind blowing that Sunday afternoon of October 1. All the townspeople were dressed in their Sunday best. Happiness Trail echoed with the sound of wind and horse hooves heading toward Precious Blood Church.

Mr. Pearlman's heart was filled with excitement, nervousness, and happiness. He would be making a very important announcement at the fellowship dinner today.

As usual, Pastor stood by the doors greeting his congregation. As he stood by the open doors, he noticed

Candy Apple pulling a new wagon. Anthony and Ruth sat comfortably inside it. Ruth greeted Pastor with a smile, Anthony with a handshake. They slid into the pew next to Amy.

Next to arrive at church was the Miller family. Holly's belly was round with child. Her face had a radiant glow. Holly's eyes sparkled with the Hopes of an expectant mother. The Miller family quietly entered the church and sat in their pew.

Summer and Adam were next. Summer was bundled that day; she had been fighting a cold all week. Sister, Forest, Anna, and the children arrived together, as well as Old Doc and the other medical staff.

Mr. Pearlman soon followed. His eyes filled with all the excitement of a child.

The hour was getting late, and Sara had not arrived yet at the church. No one was frantically worried about her. Turner said, "She probably just needed to rest today." They all agreed he was probably right.

Pastor started the service with a simple prayer that Sara would get the rest she needed. He then asked everyone to turn to Revelations. Pastor then spoke of his own revelations he had seen in the changes of the town. Everyone listened to Pastor's words. They were riveted to his sermon.

Nurse Lilly sang "Faith of our Fathers" as Mr. Pepper played the organ. Pastor then blessed the congregation and closed with a prayer.

The wind was picking up a little as everyone walked to the fellowship hall. They made small talk with each other until they reached the hall.

Helena and Sister shared the cooking responsibilities that week.

Turner asked Old Doc if he would like to go with him to check up on Sara. He agreed. Mr. Pearlman overheard the conversation. He interrupted by saying, "Gentlemen, may I come too? I'd like to share the news. I am about to share with everyone with Sara as well." Turner gladly welcomed Mr. Pearlman along.

Pastor blessed the food; everyone happily munched on his or her food. They exchanged Sunday pleasantries with one another.

After they were done eating, Mr. Pearlman took the floor and announced his big news. With a mile-long smile, he said, "I am pleased and honored to announce that the dance studio is one week away from being complete and the medical clinic is two months away from being finished. "

"Wonderful! Oh that is wonderful," Ruth said with a cheer.

Old Doc said, "We will dedicate all our work at the new clinic to the ultimate healer, Christ our Lord."

With Mr. Pearlman's exciting news, Turner bowed his head, all the others followed, and he said these beautiful words from Isaiah: "Behold, I will create new heaven and a new earth. The former things will not be remembered, nor will they come to mind. But be glad and rejoice forever in what I create." All were very excited in what Mr. Pearlman spoke of.

Sister's fears were fleeting in that moment of celebration as well. Helena could not contain her excitement and started dancing with Mr. Frederick. Everyone caught the excitement bug; they burst out in song, dance, and praise.

Mr. Pearlman then said, "Turner, Doc, and I must be going. We want to tell Sara the good news." Everyone bid his or her farewell. Like three giddy teenagers, each one on a horse raced each other down Happiness Trail, each one trying to get to Sara's door first.

Turner arrived at Sara's doorstep first. But he did patiently wait for the other men to catch up. When Doc and Mr. Pearlman caught up to him, Turner gave a happy knock on Sara's door.

Sara called out in a sleepy voice, "Come in!" When the men entered the front door, they found Sara wearing a long flannel nightgown, red bathrobe, and slippers. Her hair was not yet combed and her face unwashed.

"Excuse us, Sara, we did not mean to disturb your Sunday slumber," Turner said. Sara then let out a congested cough.

"Sara, you don't feel well?" Old Doc asked in a fatherly voice.

"I am just fighting a cold," Sara replied.

"You let me be the judge of that," Old Doc said. Turner could see the worry in Doc's eyes. "If you gentlemen would excuse me, I would like to take Sara back to her bedroom and exam her for a moment," Old Doc explained.

"But Doc, I am fine," Sara objected.

"Yes, but it will give me peace of mind to listen to your chest," Old Doc said. Turner and Mr. Pearlman granted Old Doc his request. Turner could tell by the length of time Old Doc spent with Sara it was more than just a cold.

A little while later, Old Doc emerged from Sara's bedroom without Sara. "Sara is resting. Mr. Pearlman, you may tell Sara the news, but please don't stay long," Old Doc said with a deep, worried voice.

"Is she okay?" Turner questioned. Old Doc eyes hung low.

"Sara has pneumonia. She needs a lot of rest," he explained.

"Is she going to be all right?" Mr. Pearlman asked of his new friend.

"Yes, but she needs lots of rest," Old Doc replied.

Mr. Pearlman then left to tell Sara the wonderful news. Suddenly they heard Sara scream. Old Doc and Turner raced to her bedroom.

"Sara, what is it?" Turner said with heavy breath.

"I am so sorry I scared you. I just can't believe in one week I will be running my own dance school," Sara replied.

"Yes, Sara, but you need to get some rest so you can get well," Turner said.

Sara lightened their worried moods by saying, "Don't worry. Papa Doc is going to make sure I get well."

Old Doc smiled and then said, "I will stay with Sara tonight. Turner, can you tell Nurse Lilly that I need my medical bag and herbs here tonight?

Turner could tell that Sara's pneumonia was more serious then Old Doc was letting on. Turner agreed to get the word to the nurse. He then kissed Sara on her forehead.

Mr. Pearlman said goodbye to Sara and the other men and left. Old Doc was glad. He wanted to talk to Turner alone.

"How serious is it?" Turner asked, concerned.

Old Doc replied, "After major surgery, any kind of infection is serious. Please rush to tell Nurse Lilly, Doc Friendsmore, and Doc Olson to come here immediately."

"Doc, do you need me back here too?" Turner asked.

"No, but please get the word to Pastor to pray for Sara," Old Doc said with a heavy heart.

"I will get the word to everyone as quickly as possible," Turner promised.

Mr. Pearlman had an urgent feeling in his heart to speed up his crew to get the dance studio finished. Before he went back to his apartment, he decided he would go see his crew. When he arrived at the job site, his foreman gave him the surprise of his life. "It is finished," the foreman said.

"It is?" Mr. Pearlman said with a look of disbelief.

"Yes, look at it yourself," the foreman said.

When Mr. Pearlman opened the beautiful double French doors, a tear fell from his eye. The first room he entered into was Sara's office. It was a big room painted pink; it had a big white desk, a rocking chair, a beautiful day bed that was sitting in front of a picture window. When he opened the adjoining door and stepped in, he entered the first ballroom. Over the doorway was a hand-painted sign that said, "God bless all the feet that enter here." It was made by Mr. Frederick. The ballroom was something from someone's dream. It was covered by oak floors. It had a big bar attached to the walls, and so the dancers could do their stretches. All around the room there were mirrors. The next ballroom was a little smaller in size but just as elegant and beautiful. Off the second ballroom was a door leading to a beautiful butterfly garden. It was filled with roses, beautiful colorful butterflies, and humming birds.

Mr. Pearlman ran outside to his crew. "What a fine job you all did," he said to compliment his crew. "You are all dismissed, and you will all be getting a big bonus." The men cheered.

Chapter 22

Turner raced toward town. "Old God, help Sara. Help Sara find her way," he kept praying. He arrived and quickly told Nurse Lilly and the doctors about Sara's condition.

Nurse Lilly frantically grabbed the herbs while the other two doctors grabbed other medical supplies. Turner helped them.

Turner then ran to get Pastor. The hour was very late when he arrived at Pastor's doorstep. With heavy breath, he knocked on the pastor's door. The pastor opened the door with his bedclothes on. As Turner spoke, he could hear the urgency in Turner's voice. The voices of Turner and Pastor awoke Amy Carrie. The three of them began to pray.

It was a dire situation at Sara's house when Nurse Lilly and the other doctors arrived. The look on Old Doc's face when he opened the door to let them in was the only explanation they needed. With grim eyes, Old Doc said, "Sara now has a high fever, and her breathing is very labored." The doctors were professionals, so they did not show any worry or dismay when they entered Sara's bedroom.

Sara's eyes were glazed over by the high fever. She was talking in riddles that neither Old Doc nor the other medical staff could understand. Nurse Lilly prepared a special mustard rub and applied it to Sara's chest. Doc Friendsmore opened Sara's mouth slightly and poured in two teaspoons of cough syrup. Doc Olson used a special vapor machine to make the air in Sara's room moist and cool. He Hoped it would help Sara's breathing. Old Doc applied wet compressors to Sara's head in Hopes of lowering her temperature. After a few passing hours, Sara's temperature was still climbing. The doctors and nurse pulled from their guts all their medical wisdom. They decided to pack Sara in cold ice. With any luck, it would bring down her fever.

Doc Olson quickly filled a metal tub with ice and cold water. Doc Friendsmore and Old Doc gently lowered Sara into the tub. Nurse Lilly gently rubbed down her body with the ice-cold water. After a few moments, Old Doc rechecked Sara's temperature. "

"It's not working," he said. He knew in his heart Sara was not out of the woods yet.

Doc Friendsmore said, "Now we must get Sara out of this water before her body goes in to shock."

Old Doc lifted her out of the metal tub. Nurse Lilly dried off her cold limp body. Then she wrapped her in towels and a warm, cozy blanket. They laid Sara back on her bed.

"Let's find more pillows to prop up her head. It will make her breathing easier," Old Doc suggested. Nurse Lilly looked around for more pillows. She could not find any. She rolled up a wool blanket and stuck it under the pillow to raise Sara's head.

The pale moonlight hid behind the rising morning sun. Sara survived the night. Sara, in a frail voice, asked Old Doc for a sip of water.

"You gave us quite a scare, dear Sara," Doc Friendsmore said, clutching Sara's hand in his.

"I'm not going anywhere," Sara said.

"Still, Sara, you need to rest," Old Doc said, lifting her head to let her sip the water.

Turner gathered all the townspeople at church in the middle of the night to pray for Sara. Helena, Turner, Ruth, and Mr. Frederick left the church at the crack of dawn to check on Sara's condition.

When they arrived at Sara's door, Nurse Lilly greeted them. Helena ran to her,

"How is she? Did she … ?" Helena's voice trailed off.

"She is resting now," Nurse Lilly said.

"May we see her?" Turner asked.

"You will have to check with the doctors," Nurse Lilly replied. Just then Old Doc heard their voices.

"Helena and Ruth may, but I think you gentlemen should remain outside," Old Doc said in a stern voice.

Helena and Ruth were led by Nurse Lilly to Sara's room. They were both given strict orders not to show their worry in front of Sara. Ruth and Helena fought back tears. When they entered Sara's bedroom, they saw Sara awake, but in a semi-conscious state. With the touch of Helena's hand on Sara's face, Sara seemed to become more aware.

Kim made coffee and toast for everyone at church. Everyone was praying. They all wanted to go to Sara's house but were waiting for word that she could receive visitors.

"Gentlemen, I must tell you Sara is still in a very dangerous time. Her surgery was just a short six months ago. We must pray for Sara really hard now." Old Doc's voice cracked with the first tear falling from his eyes.

"Doc, what else can we do to help?" asked Mr. Frederick.

"Pray, then pray, then pray some more," was all Old Doc could say.

After a short visit with Sara, Helena and Ruth made their way out of Sara's bedroom. They talked outside in whispers so Sara would not hear. Old Doc instructed them that they had an important job of spiritual medicine.

"Prayer is the most powerful force and the strongest medicine," Nurse Lilly said.

Turner, Helena, Ruth, and Mr. Frederick promised to lead the rest of Sara's friends on the battlefield of praying for Sara's health. Meanwhile, Old Doc and the others promised to use their medical wisdom and healing hands to heal Sara's broken body.

Turner said he would be back later to check on Sara. Old Doc said it would be best that Turner be the one messenger between the doctors and the rest of the town.

Turner, Ruth, Helena, and Mr. Frederick arrived back at the church and shared the news of Sara's health with everyone. Turner led everyone in prayer.

Holly cried out, "Sara will be all right. She just has to be!"

Little Ronnie held his wife tightly in his arms while she sobbed.

Sister Victoria yelled, "This is all my fault! I knew we were pushing Sara much too hard, and I didn't say anything to stop it."

"Sister, listen to me. It's not anyone's fault. Sara has lived more of her life in these past six months than she has the past four years," Pastor gently said.

"Stop it, all of you! You are talking like Sara is dying. She is not going to die!" Helena shouted.

"Friends, listen! Listen to me! We are all prayer warriors for Sara now. Sara is in God's hands. God has a plan for Sara. He knew her heart even before he formed her body. He has caught every tear that Sara has cried. He will not let anything happen to Sara," Turner calmly stated. With Turner's touching words, a sudden peace came over the room.

Pastor then suggested that everyone go home and get some rest and meet back at the church in the afternoon.

Ruth then said, "Yes, Pastor. Poor Anna and Forest have been here all night with these babies. They need to be in their warm bed sleeping."

Anthony placed his hand on his wife's shoulder. "Yes, Ruth you are right. Holly Amber also needs her rest." They all agreed to go home and meet back at the church later on.

Mr. Frederick, Ronnie, Turner, and Little Ronnie caught up on their farm chores they could not do that morning. Helena, Kim, and Holly prepared food to share with everyone at church. When the men finished with their chores and the women finished cooking, they took a catnap, but everyone was too worried to sleep.

Ruth and Anthony took Sister home with them. They knew if she was home alone, all she would do was cry and worry.

"Mr. Pearlman told us that Sara's dance studio was finally complete and now this happens." Sister cried on Ruth's shoulder.

"It will be all right, Sister," Ruth said.

Summer could not bear to look at the tutus hanging in

her sewing room as she and Adam arrived home. Summer cried herself to sleep in Adam's arms.

Forest, Anna, and the children were so exhausted they fell asleep right away.

Pastor and Amy continued to pray for an hour and then took a nap as well.

Mr. Pepper felt lost. He was very glad when Mr. Pearlman invited him to come to Sara's dance studio. Mr. Pepper and Mr. Pearlman found themselves in the butterfly garden praying.

"Tell me the story again of little Hope," Mr. Pearlman said to Mr. Pepper. Mr. Pepper again shared the beautiful story of the little girl Sara met in the hospital's garden.

Chapter 23

"Nurse Lilly, why don't you go home and get some rest. Doc Olson, Old Doc, and I are here to watch over Sara," Dr. Friendsmore suggested.

"Oh, I can't sleep. Sara is like my sister. I want to be awake in case she calls my name," Nurse Lilly replied.

"Nurse Lilly, it would really be good if you took at least an hour's nap. I promise I will wake you in an hour," Old Doc said.

"Well, if you promise you won't let me sleep more than an hour, I will," Nurse Lilly responded.

Nurse Lilly sat in the rocking chair and rocked herself to sleep. Doc Friendsmore and Doc Olson caught a few ZZZs themselves.

"Doc, are you still here?" Sara said in a small, fragile, child-like voice.

"Yes, sweetness, I am here. Can I get you something?" Old Doc asked in a caring tone.

"I don't feel good, Doc. I feel sick, like I got a crushing weight on my chest," Sara said, coughing. Old Doc's worst fears were becoming a reality.

"Sara, just try to close your eyes and try to relax. I am going to fix you some chicken soup," Doc said.

Sara did close her eyes and imagined happy thoughts. She pictured herself at the dance studio.

Old Doc went in to Sara's small kitchen. He took out a small cast-iron pot and heated some chicken soup; he heated it over an open flame. When it was heated, he poured it into a small bowl. He then made Sara some earl gray tea. He placed both the bowl and the teacup on a wooden carrying tray. He brought it into Sara's bedroom. Sara was fast asleep. He did not have the heart to wake Sara.

An hour passed. Old Doc woke up the other doctors and Nurse Lilly. He made them eat some chicken soup; he then talked to them about Sara's medical condition.

"Is she awake?" Nurse Lilly quietly asked.

"No, I went to bring her something to eat, and she fell back to sleep," Old Doc said.

"After I am done eating, I will wake her and get her to eat something," Nurse Lilly said. The doctors and nurse ate their lunches in silence. After Nurse Lilly was done eating, she did as she said she would.

"How is she doing?" Doc Friendsmore asked Old Doc.

"When she was awake, she said she had a crushing pain in her chest," Old Doc responded.

"We must get her to start coughing up some phlegm; otherwise, her lungs will fill with fluid and her pneumonia will get worse," Doc Olson said.

"Yes, that is my worst fear," Old Doc admitted.

"When I was at the hospital in Paradise Gates, we had a machine that would do just that," Doc Friendsmore said.

"But right now she is too weak to be moved to the hospital there," Doc Olson said.

"Yes, we cannot move her, but maybe we can bring the machine here?" Old Doc asked, Hopeful.

"We can't. It can't be taken out of the hospital, but if we get Sara stable enough, we can bring her back to Paradise Gates," Doc Friendsmore sadly stated.

Knock, knock, the heavy sound of heavy knuckles pounding against Sara's front door. It was Turner. Old Doc met him at the front door.

"We are all on our way back to the church to pray. I just wanted to check up on Sara," Turner said with waiting breath.

Just then, Nurse Lilly came from Sara's bedroom. Old Doc invited Turner in, and then he turned his attention to Nurse Lilly.

"Did she eat?" Old Doc asked.

"Not much. Only a couple of sips. Her skin is getting wet and clammy again too. I think her fever is getting higher," Nurse Lilly stated with horror in her voice.

Old Doc, his voice filled with fear, said, "We have to get that fever to break and have to get her to start coughing up."

Before Old Doc could finish, Nurse Lilly said, "Turner, she heard you come in; she wants to talk with you."

"May I see Sara?" Turner asked her loyal band of caregivers.

Doc Friendsmore answered him by saying, "Yes, but don't stay long." Turner promised not to.

When Turner walked to Sara's bedside, he could see her face was gray. Her eyes were sunken in, and her beautiful smile was replaced by her dry, parched lips. The color of her rosy cheeks were robbed by the fever. Turner walked over to Sara. He kissed her on the forehead. Sara's shaky hand reached for his. She looked deep into his eyes. Her voice was fragile, but it was crisp and clear at the same time.

Sara said, "Turner, I know my fate is sealed. I know God will be calling me home soon. I want you to gather my friends so I can say goodbye, and I want you to promise me you will convince Old Doc to let me see my dance studio just once."

"Sara, don't say such things. You are going to be with us for a very long time," Turner said, holding back his tears and tighten his grip on Sara's hands.

"Turner, in my heart I know God speaks to you. I know you know that what I say is true. Now promise me this," Sara begged.

"Sara, please don't let doubt come into your heart. You will be with …" Turner's voice broke.

"Turner, I am not afraid to go to my eternal rest. I know God is calling me home, so please, my brother, please promise me." Turner, not trying to hide his tears any longer, promised Sara her last wish. "I want to see my dance studio tonight, Turner. Promise me," Sara said before drifting back into a feverish sleep.

Turner heart troubled and worried walked back out of Sara's bedroom to talk with Old Doc, Nurse Lilly and the other doctors. With tears burning his cheeks, he spoke to them the words Sara spoke.

"That is just the fever talking. She is not going—" Before Old Doc could finish, Doc Olson jumped in, saying, "We all know deep in our hearts Sara's fate."

Old Doc collapsed. "We can't give up!" he cried.

"We are not giving up, but we must grant Sara's wish," Nurse Lilly said.

Turner got Old Doc up. "Listen to me, Doc. If you love Sara, you must let her go in peace," Turner whispered to Old Doc.

"How am I going to let my dear Sara go?" he said with tears streaming down his face.

"God will show us how," Turner whispered softly.

It was half past four when Turner arrived back at the church with the grim news. He did not know how he was going to break the news to Sara's friends. But he had to.

When Turner walked into the church, he saw everyone in a prayer circle, tightly holding each other's hands. Pastor was reading from the book of Hebrews. Pastor read these words: "Never will I leave you, never will I forsake you, so say with confidence the Lord is my helper, I will not be afraid."

Everyone heard Turner's footsteps, so they turned around to face the doors of the church.

"How is she? How is my sister?" Helena asked, racing toward Turner. Mr. Frederick could always read the frown on Turner's face.

"Everyone needs to sit down," Turner said. Helena immediately passed out. Mr. Frederick gently fanned his wife with his hand until she opened her eyes. Then everyone sat down.

"This is not easy for me to say, nor will it be easy for you to hear. This is God's will, and you need to accept that," Turner said with a grim voice. "Sara is requesting a service tonight at the dance studio so she can say goodbye," Turner said.

"There has to be something that Old Doc and the other doctors can do for her!" Ruth cried.

"Sara has accepted her fate, and we must too," Turner calmly pointed out.

"Never! I will never let her go. You are a liar, Turner Thomas, and she is not dying!" Helena turned pounded on Turner's chest as she shouted at him.

Turner let Helena take her anger out on him. When she began weeping, she held her hand and said, "God is taking care of her."

Pastor then gently took Helena hand in his and said, "Be not afraid, Helena. God has room at his table for her." Everyone began sobbing frantically. They all held on to each other and cried together for what seemed like hours.

Little Ronnie then gently spoke these beautiful words of comfort from the book of 1 Peter: "See, I lay a stone in Zion, a chosen and precious cornerstone, and the one who trust in him shall never be put to shame."

With those words, God's faithful children were reminded to trust in his plan. Sister then finally spoke. "We must do what Sara asked of us."

Pastor and Turner led them in prayer. They prayed for strength, guidance, wisdom, and peace of heart and mind. Quietly they filed out of the small little church. They got on their horses and in their wagons and made their way down Happiness Trail to Sara's house.

Happiness Trail was covered with fall golden leaves and silver moonlight. Turner could not help but notice all the stars shining above Sara's house when everyone arrived.

Old Doc saw everyone standing outside. He knew that Sara's body was growing weaker and weaker. All that evening, Sara was fading in and out. He called Ruth and Anthony in to talk to Sara first

Anthony had to carry Ruth to Sara's bedside. Ruth's knees would not allow her to take the final step to say goodbye to Sara. Sara spoke in whispers.

"Aunt Ruth, Uncle Anthony, you must promise me you will carry on with our plan. My dance studio is the legacy I leave this earth."

Ruth could not speak, so Anthony said, "We promise." Ruth and Anthony said their final goodbyes to Sara.

Holly and Little Ronnie were called in next. Holly put on her bravest face, but Sara could see the fear behind her eyes. "Holly, I leave you my dance studio to teach the gift of dance, to share with others the joy we feel when we both dance," Sara said.

"Sara, you are not leaving us, so don't." Sara did not let Holly finish; instead, she looked at Little Ronnie and said, "Take care of her."

Little Ronnie responded, saying, "I will, and if we have a girl, we will teach her to dance as gracefully as you." Sara managed a small smile.

Sara said, "I need to rest for a little while, but I will not leave until I say goodbye to the others and see my dance studio." Just then Old Doc walked in. Sara's fever was getting higher. It was getting harder for her to breath.

Everyone was outside praying. Nurse Lilly burst into song to lift everyone's spirits and give Sara courage. The harmony of their voices filled the little valley like angels from heaven.

Old Doc let Sara sleep when she awoke. She began to request to see her friends again.

Adam, Summer, Kim, and Ronnie entered Sara's room next. Sara had a special request of them. "Promise you will let me wear my dance slippers to heaven," Sara asked. Summer and Kim could not bear the thought. They began crying uncontrollably, and Sara did too.

Sister was the next friend to see Sara. Sister made Sara laugh. She revealed stories of her wild days as a young girl.

Pastor and Amy Carrie prayed with Sara and Sister. Sara made them promise to take care of Morning Dew. Forest, Anna, and the children said goodbye to Sara next.

Mr. Pearlman, Mr. Pepper, and Nurse Lilly went to see Sara next. Sara gave them heartfelt thanks for changing her life. She then asked Nurse Lilly to sing to her. "Sing to me like an angel," Sara said. Nurse Lilly sang Be Not Afraid." Sara's eyes brightened as Nurse Lilly sang.

Sara then spoke to Old Doc, Doc Friendsmore, and Doc Olson. "Don't blame yourselves. You did all you could do for me." Old Doc squeezed her hand.

"I love you, my dear Sara," he said.

"I love you too," Sara said.

Helena and Mr. Frederick were next. Sara and Helena left nothing unspoken between them. They spoke of love, life, dreams, fears, and things only sisters could share of the heart.

Turner then made his way to the bedroom. Although he tried to be strong, his unspeakable sadness fell with every tear. "Don't cry, Turner. You filled me with happiness from the moment I met you. You changed my life. I just wish we would have had more time together. Turner, don't you realize what you have given me? The little girl I met in the hospital gave me Hope. When Anna's daughters were born and she named her one baby Sara Faith, she gave me faith. But you, Turner Thomas, gave me love, and remember what the good book says—'faith, love, and

Hope, but the greatest of these is love.'" Sara struggled to take a breath. She closed her beautiful eyes.

Sara opened her eyes. When she opened them, she was looking into Turner's beautiful eyes. "Turner, I had the strangest dream," Sara said.

"Look around you, Sara. What do you see?" Turner asked.

When Sara looked around, she wasn't sure if she was still dreaming or not. She saw a beautiful rainbow outstretched as far as the naked eye could see. She saw doves flying around; she saw beautiful waterfalls running into a tranquil stream. Her nose smelled the finest jasmine and roses. Her ears heard a sound she had never heard before. It was the sound of singing, and the voices blended and harmonized into one.

"Turner, how come I don't feel sick?" Sara asked, puzzled.

"Sara, you are in heaven," Turner said softly.

"Heaven? How can that be? I was sick, not you. When I last saw you, you were taking care of me," Sara said in an even more puzzled voice.

Turner smiled and said, "My dear, dear Sara, I am an angel. I was sent down to earth to help you and your friends."

"An angel?" Sara said, confused.

"Yes, I am an angel. Sara, please come with me. There are some people that have been waiting a really long time to see your smile again," Turner went on to say.

Sara followed Turner, filled with excitement, joy, and peace.

"Mom, Dad, Grandpa Miller, you're here! You are

here. This really is not a dream. This is heaven!" Sara ran and embraced them.

Sara then felt a tug on her leg. When she looked down, she saw little Hope. She picked up Hope and hugged her with a tight-fisted hug. Sara then asked, "Hope, are you an angel too?"

Hope replied, "No, Sara, but I am your friend." Sara smiled.

"Turner, is Larry here?" Sara asked, Hopeful. Sara was suddenly filled with the warmest feeling she ever had.

"Sara, of course I am here. Your love and forgiveness gave me wings." Larry put his arms around Sara. Sara was filled with a sweeping overpowering feeling of love. For the first time ever, she was able to read Larry's heart.

Grandma Miller then said, "This is what true love is."

Turner then said, "Come, there is someone else you must meet." Sara followed Turner. Turner led her to Jesus. Sara dropped to her knees and started to cry.

Jesus said, "My dear child, don't cry." Jesus wrapped her in an embrace of shelter, tenderness, and warmth.

Sara said, "I am crying tears of joy." She looked up at Jesus for the first time ever. She was able to see her own beauty in his eyes. Jesus said, "Sara, you have always been beautiful to me."

Sara asked Jesus, "What will happen to all my friends? Will they be okay?"

Jesus replied, "My children pray to me all the time for the desires of their hearts. Sometimes I tell them the answer is no; sometimes I tell them the answer is yes, but sometimes my children are the answer to each other's prayers. Sara, you and your friends learned that love means sacrifice. Forgiveness means grace, and sometimes out of the tragedy of suffering comes Hope. You, my dear Sara, have learned the greatest lesson of all. Love never fails, and I will give you beauty for your ashes. Your friends have faith in me; that's all they will ever need."

Sara felt very comforted.

Jesus then told Sara the future of her friends. Holly and Little Ronnie would have a little girl that would become a great ballerina. Ruth and Anthony would successfully run the dance studio. Helena and Mr. Frederick would go on to adopt a brother and sister from Poland. Pastor and Amy would grow in their faith. Sister Victoria would live out her last days as a midwife. The new clinic would be a success and help a lot of people. And the rest of her friends would live happy lives.

Jesus then showed Sara her dance studio from heaven. Sara noticed she was wearing her dance slippers. She began dancing joyfully for Jesus. Larry then gave her a pair of wings.